An Involuntary Spy
Kenneth Eade

For my dear Valentina
The Love of my Life

When a lie becomes the truth,
The truth becomes a lie – Samm Simpson, GMO Activist

CHAPTER ONE

The headlines of every newspaper and every Internet news service ran the same story. His story; the story of Seth Rogan, 45-year-old genetic biologist. Some were calling him a whistleblower.

Society tends to stick labels on everything and everyone. The label that is given to you will stick with you for a lifetime, especially in these days of the fledging Internet, which is swallowing up and replacing traditional journalism with real-time news. The separation that once was between news and opinion has blurred, and the two have bled into one another.

Some were calling him a traitor. The President of the United States said he was wanted for "espionage" and "aiding our enemies." Somewhere between his good intentions and unselfish acts, he had become the "bad guy." Espionage was always something that Seth had read about in novels or watched in the movies. He had never experienced it in real life... until now. He didn't feel like James Bond. He knew he couldn't step off this Aeroflot non-stop flight from Washington to Moscow clean-shaven, shoot ten bad guys who were on his tail, and then relax in bed with a beautiful female Russian spy, sipping on a vodka martini, shaken not stirred.

Seth stirred uneasily in his seat as the Captain made an announcement over the PA system.

"Ladies and gentlemen, this is your Captain speaking. I'm afraid we have had a bit of a change in routing. We're about 150 kilometers east of Kiev and have been directed by air traffic control to set down here. There is no cause for alarm – it's only routine. After about an hour or so, we'll be back on our way to Moscow."

The 777 lurched as the passengers moaned and groaned. They had already endured a long flight, preceded by a lengthy mechanical delay. They were tired..... Tired of the bad food, tired of the uncomfortable seats, just plain tired.

No cause for alarm? Maybe not for them, but, in Seth's case, there was definitely cause for alarm. The last time he had checked the Soviet Union had long been disbanded, and Ukraine and Russia were separate countries; but, apparently, the Ukraine was now the 51st state of the United States because the U.S. was forcing a Russian plane to land there. Seth's heart beat as fast as a crack addict's, almost thumping out of his chest. He clutched tightly to his briefcase, even though he had long since spilled all the beans by electronic upload. He held no more secrets on him to reveal – except one. The one without scientific backup and peer reviewed studies... the scariest one, the secret that he held onto to keep him alive. The plane began its descent into Kiev, and, with every air bump, Seth's panic renewed. He became nauseous.

This was it. He was screwed, doomed to spend the rest of his life in jail, or, even worse, to be shot on sight. Well, he deserved it for what he had done. Let the show begin.

Seth looked out the window at the cold, harsh landscape. It was barren and dry, a forest of a million tiny sticks. He tried to keep his mind clear. He knew what to do.

The plane touched down on the tarmac. The purser robotically performed her landings "voice over" on the PA system.

"Welcome to Kiev, ladies and gentlemen, where local time is approximately 6:30 a.m. We will be taxying for a while so please keep seated with your seatbelts on until the aircraft has parked at the gate."

Yeah, like Kiev was just where Seth wanted to be. How could this happen? He was so careful. He didn't waste any time – got right out of there. How did they know he was on this plane? Russia didn't have an extradition treaty with the United States, and he had chosen Moscow as his route of escape. It was easy to get a non-stop flight from the states, and the government didn't tag you when you were leaving, only when you were going back into the states. He was naïve to think they would let him bolt.

"Ladies and gentlemen, it will be necessary for you to deplane here. Please take all of your belongings with you and hold on to your boarding passes so you can re-board the aircraft. Please have passports out and open for police inspection at the door of the aircraft," said the purser.

The passengers fumbled for their belongings and trudged down the aisle toward the front of the plane. Seth stayed put, clutching his briefcase. A cute, blonde flight attendant came up to him, smiling.

"Sir you'll have to deplane here. It's only for about one hour."

"I'm not going anywhere."

"Sir?"

The poor flight attendant didn't know what to do. Her smile faded into a frown.

"Please call the Captain."

"Sir, please, I..."

"Call the Captain. I need to speak to the Captain."

The flustered attendant went to the intercom phone and picked it up. Within minutes, as the plane continued to empty, a pilot approached.

"Sir, what is the problem?"

"Are you the Captain?"

"I'm the First Officer. Now are you going to tell me why you refuse to leave the aircraft?"

"They're looking for me. I'm the reason they forced the plane to land here. My name is Seth Rogan, and I'm a political refugee. I've petitioned for asylum from the Russian government, and the Ukraine has nothing to do with it. I won't surrender to anyone except a representative of the Russian Embassy."

"Sir, I..."

"Did you hear what I said?" Seth nervously clutched his briefcase.

"Sir, what is in the briefcase?"

"Call the Russian Embassy. Seth Rogan. I'm not leaving the plane except with them. I'm not coming out. Period."

The First Officer turned and left. Now the plane was almost entirely empty. After a few moments, he returned with another pilot.

"Sir," he said, "I'm Captain Davidoff. I understand you have some kind of diplomatic issue, but can you tell me what is in the case?"

"Have you called the Russian Embassy?"

"Yes, we have, sir. Now can you please tell me what you have in there?"

"Why are you so curious?"

"Because, sir, the way you're holding it and sweating – you look very nervous."

"You'd be nervous, too, if you were about to be taken by the CIA."

"CIA? Sir, I don't know what you're talking about, but..."

"Of course, you don't. I'll leave your plane but only with an official from the Russian Embassy."

The Captain turned to talk to his First Officer and they spoke to each other in Russian. *"Is the crew off?"*

"Yes."

"Good. I'm not getting off until I find out what's happening."

"I'm with you."

Two armed police, accompanied by a man in a gray business suit, Jack Singer, one of the CIA's men in Kiev, approached them. He spoke.

"What is your name?" he asked in a typical American accent, Midwest probably.

"What's yours?" said Seth, facetiously.

"That's not important. May I see some identification sir?"

"I don't have any."

"What happened to it?"

"It fell in the toilet."

Singer turned to one of the armed policeman and ordered, "Go look in the toilet."

The Captain interrupted. "Nobody is going anywhere in my plane without asking me first."

"Sir," said Singer, "This is a matter of national security."

"Which nation?" Seth chimed in. "I didn't know the United States government had the right to force a plane down in international airspace."

"Neither did I," said the Captain. "This is a Russian plane, and that's not what I was told. What's going on here?"

"I'm sorry Captain. I can't tell you. It's on a need-to-know basis," said Singer.

"Well, I happen to be the pilot in charge, and I need to know. I'm responsible for this plane and everyone on it."

"Captain, this is not about you. Sir, I'm asking you again, what is your name?"

"Don't you know?" Seth replied. "I'm Barney Rubble, you know, Fred's best friend?"

"I don't think you realize sir that you are in a lot of trouble."

In Russian, a voice from the front of the plane boomed out, "I don't think you realize, Jack, that the CIA has no jurisdiction here, and this man is under my protection."

The voice was from Yuri Streltsov, a strapping young Russian man of about 30 with a neck so thick it looked like his head was directly attached to his shoulders, biceps like Arnold Schwarzenegger, and not the best command of the English language.

"Hello, Yuri," said Singer.

Yuri flashed his badge at the police, and they nodded.

"Let's go, Barney," Yuri said, as he made a sweeping motion with his hand for Seth to come. Singer smiled slyly at them as they exited the plane.

"You may be able to walk through this airport, Yuri, but I can't guarantee you safe passage once you leave," said Singer.

"Oh Jack, I didn't know you cared," said Yuri.

"What did he mean?" said Seth to Yuri.

"He means they have a team of assassins waiting outside, and they have no problem killing me - along with you – because, after we are dead, they will disappear, and our bodies will never be found."

"Great, but you have men too, right?"

"Just me."

"Just you?"

"Don't worry. Here, put this on."

Yuri handed him a heavy, gray vest with straps, like a life-jacket.

"What's that?"

"Bullet-proof vest."

CHAPTER 2

As they exited the plane, Yuri made it clear to the police to back off – this was not their affair. Seth looked back and could see Jack Singer on his radio, and it didn't look like he was calling his guys to tell them they lost the game. He had no reason to trust this Yuri Streltsov, but his choices were limited; liberty, albeit temporary, or death. He chose liberty.

Just outside the jetway, Yuri shoved Seth through a door with a red "circle sign" on it that Seth supposed meant, "No entry," or something like it.

"Can you run?" Yuri said.

"I'm still trying to put on this vest."

"You wanted to be spy. Learn to multi-task."

"I never wanted to be a spy. I just wanted to warn people about ..."

"We talk later. Have to go now." Yuri grabbed Seth by the shoulders, buckled on the vest, and gave him a shove. "Run!"

Seth ran. Following Yuri, he ran as fast as he could. He ran so fast he could feel the stinging sweat pouring into his eyes. Through one door, then another, down one set of stairs so fast his feet barely brushed each step, and then through a tunnel. Finally, they smashed through a set of double doors. Seth felt the shock of the cold, outside air filling his lungs but only for a second, as he was shoved into an already moving, black Mercedes - head first, like a criminal under arrest or a kidnap victim.

Yuri jumped in next to him, gun in hand, and the Mercedes took off through the parking lot and out the gated exit. The driver accelerated as the man next to him began yelling something in Russian. He looked panicked.

"What is he saying?" asked Seth.

"He says they are after us."

Seth looked in the rear window but didn't see anything unusual. "How does he know?"

"Look."

Just then, not one, but two cars emerged from the parking lot; the first one breaking through the gate arm, and the other right behind it. They were both swerving in and out of the line of traffic like maniacs, which is what their own driver was now doing.

"We will be at embassy in ten minutes," said Yuri.

"Can't we call the police – for backup?"

"Look, Seth, you are not very good spy, are you? Police have no official business to stop us, but they are not going to help us. Once we get to embassy, Russian Special Forces – Spetsnaz – they will be all backup we need."

"Why don't they come now?"

"This is Ukraine, no longer same country as Russia. On embassy ground is only place they can act."

The pursuing car behind them on the right, a black Mercedes jeep, sped up to catch them and played a game of tag with their car, which lurched forward to avoid being pinned.

"Windows are bulletproof but get down anyway," yelled Yuri. Seth obeyed.

Their driver swerved evasively as the pursuing jeep caught up. The driver of the jeep motioned angrily for them to pull over. Then the guy in the passenger side of Seth's car pulled his gun out, rolled down the window, and fired back their answer.

"What's going on?" asked Seth, hearing the gunshots and peeking out of his hiding place.

"He trying to shoot tires."

The pursuing jeep swerved, and its occupants shot back multiple shots, which Seth could hear pinging against the metal sides of their car.

Yuri pushed Seth down further behind the driver's seat, yelling "Get down!" and rolled down his window, shooting at the jeep. One shot, two shots, then the third blew out the jeep's left front tire, and the jeep lost control, hurling into oncoming traffic. Most of the cars swerved out of the way like a synchronized swim, but a truck hit the rear side of the jeep, sending it into an uncontrolled spin, and another car smashed into its passenger side, completely crushing the jeep and most likely its occupants. The second pursuing car, a silver Mercedes sedan, was stuck behind the resulting jam.

"What happens when they find dead CIA agents in that jeep with guns?" said Seth, rising from his hiding place.

"All will be clean. There will be no guns, no agents. Just American tourists involved in traffic accident," said Yuri.

Just as it seemed they were out of danger, the silver Mercedes emerged and pushed itself up on the shoulder of the road, away from the jammed-up cars.

"They're back," yelled Seth.

Their driver accelerated, weaving through cars, making evasive moves.

"How many times do I say get down!" said Yuri, and pushed Seth down again. "We are almost there."

The silver Mercedes was again on their tail. Seth's driver floored it, swerving into the right lane and almost hitting the car in front of them. He came right up on the rear bumper of another car, hit the brakes, downshifted, and powered around it.

"Embassy is here," said Yuri.

One more screeching sharp right turn, and they were at the gates of the embassy, which was opened by two Spetsnaz soldiers. The gates closed behind them, and the pursuing silver Mercedes rolled by slowly.

Yuri was an agent of the Russian Federal Security Service, or FSB. His assignment was Seth – to keep him alive, deliver him to Russia, and monitor his ongoing safety pending the decision on his application for asylum. So far, it was a task he had not failed. As their Mercedes entered the grounds of the Russian Embassy, several armed guards took their watch posts behind it. A steel garage door opened and closed behind the Mercedes and Yuri ushered Seth inside.

Yuri took Seth into a waiting room. The room and the entire building was a classic throwback to the days of Imperial Russia. Original oil paintings hung from the richly wallpapered walls, framed by wood cornices. Seth sat down in one of the classic, cushy French armchairs that decorated the room. He was offered water by a beautiful Ukrainian brunette, which he gladly accepted.

After gulping a fair share of water, Seth was led into the Ambassador's office. The Ambassador, a man in his early 60s with graying hair, met Seth with an outstretched hand. "Good morning, Mr. Rogan, I am Gregori Petrov, the Ambassador to the Ukraine."

"Good morning."

"I know that Kiev was not your final destination, but we would like to welcome you here just the same."

"Thank you, Ambassador. It seems I owe you my life," said Seth.

"Gratitude is not necessary. Your safety is of utmost concern to us. On the other hand, your government seems intent to harm you, Mr. Rogan. Have you decided what to do with your documents?"

"First, I want to make sure the public knows the dangers of genetically engineered foods and how the government allowed them into the market despite the danger."

"And the other matter?"

"That I have not decided yet. Can you tell me the status of my petition for asylum?"

"That is being considered by the President himself right now, but we have been instructed to give you safe passage to Russia and to protect you during your stay there. Mr. Streltsov will be your point of contact, and I can assure you he is very good at what he does."

"I have seen that."

"You will dine with me tonight, here at the embassy, and we have prepared one of the apartments for your brief stay with us. Tomorrow we will escort you to the airport for your flight to Moscow with a full diplomatic motorcade of security."

"Thank you."

The Russians had always been the enemies to Seth as long as he had known, although the U.S. never had the war with them that everyone had anticipated. They had always been the enemies in every movie, and he remembered one day in high school when the entire school was ushered into the gym for an assembly where they were lectured on the dangers of the "evil empire." "*Their newspaper is called Pravda, which means truth,*" they had said, "*but it's filled with lies.*" Seth had no reason to trust his new protectors, but his choices were limited to them, and them alone, at this point. He had willingly placed himself, ironically, in the hands of the enemy.

CHAPTER 3

Seth sat in the green room of the studio of the news channel, *Russia Today*, waiting for his interview. He had selected *Russia Today* to tell his story because they were a new, up-and-coming international news channel that broadcast news of Russian and international interest in English. Seth twiddled his thumbs together nervously. He had come a long way to tell his story and now the time was finally upon him. There was no turning back. A pretty, blonde girl came in to take him to his interview, while another girl powdered his face a bit more and hooked up a lapel microphone.

"Are you ready?" she asked.

"Ready now as I ever will be," said Seth.

The blonde walked him into the studio. "This is Pavel Kargin," said the girl. Pavel shook Seth's hand.

"You're a brave man," he said, with a friendly smile. "I will try not to traumatize you any more than necessary."

Pavel took his seat and began the interview. "Hello, this is Pavel Kargin reporting from Moscow with an exclusive interview with Seth Rogan, an ex-Germinat scientist who has fled the United States and sought refuge here in Russia. Good to have you here, Seth."

"Good to be here, Pavel."

"Please tell our audience why you have selected Russia and why you thought it was dangerous for you to remain in America?"

"I chose Russia, not because I'm a traitor, but because there was no way I could tell this story unless I kept my freedom. While I was working at Germinat, I came across some government documents that prove the U.S. government knew that our genetically engineered foods are unsafe."

"Can you explain to our audience what a genetically engineered food is?"

"A genetically engineered organism, or GMO, as it is commonly referred to, is a plant or animal of one species whose DNA is genetically altered in a laboratory by inserting genes from a different species in order to breed a trait in that organism that does not exist in nature."

"Haven't farmers been doing that for many years? They make a crop of corn, for example, that is sweeter than other types of corn."

"No, what you are talking about is natural breeding within the same species. Combining one strain of corn that has a trait we want with another strain, like breeding dogs or horses, is not genetic engineering. What we do in genetic engineering is to take a gene from the DNA of one species and insert it into the DNA of a completely different species. This is a type of breeding that could never occur in nature. For example, the first genetically engineered crop was a tomato that could stand cold weather without freezing. We took a gene from a fish that lived in cold waters and inserted it into the DNA of the tomato. The result was a freeze-proof tomato."

" Genes of a fish go into genes of a tomato?"

"Yes."

"What is the danger in that?"

"The danger is that we don't really know all the consequences of what could happen. Did you ever see the movie 'The Fly?'"

"Yes."

"In 'The Fly,' when the scientist tested his teleporter by using himself as the test subject, his genes were "spliced" with the genes of a fly that was in the teleporter with him. All kinds of unexpected things began happening to his body, and he eventually turned into a monster. When we splice a gene from an animal or a bacteria into the gene of a plant, we don't really know everything that will happen. Evolution has had millions of years to work with the present species that we know on earth. Because of the genetic engineering process, which is very new at the moment, the GMO plant we make today could produce toxins or even viruses that we have never seen, and we may not be able to control them. The government says that if the genetically engineered food looks like conventional food, then it is safe, but that ignores what is happening on a cellular level."

"You are saying that, even if the food looks the same, the dangers are hidden inside?"

"Exactly. The government reports that I obtained from my company state that the project I was working on, for example, produces a food which is not safe for human consumption, but it has been approved anyway. We were taking a gene from the DNA of a bacteria that is a natural insecticide that makes the stomach of an insect explode and planting it into the DNA of a corn crop. That way, the corn will produce its own insecticide, and, when insects eat it, they will die. The problem is that the corn produces a poison which is far more potent than the bacteria found naturally. In the process, we also use a potent plant virus, which is similar to the AIDS virus, to stimulate the production of the toxin. It could lie dormant and reactivate later or produce an even different virus that we have never seen. We use antibiotic resistant genes in the process, which could cause resistance to very common antibiotics, leaving us open to all kinds of bacterial diseases."

"Toxins, viruses, antibiotic resistance – that doesn't sound like safe things to be putting into our food."

"Exactly. That is what the reports from the United States government state, and my company, Germinat, has succeeded in burying those reports from public view."

"It's a good thing that these foods are not yet on the market."

"They are though. They have already been approved and are in 70% of the processed foods eaten in America and almost all animal feed."

"That's why you left the states and are afraid of prosecution because you have these government reports that they don't want to make public."

"Not exactly."

"What then?"

"They're after me because I have a top-secret government report that details experiments using the same genetic engineering to make biological weapons."

"Are they making biological weapons with this technology now?"

"Not yet, but I don't think it is something that should be done. The current technology being experimented on is for the so-called "war on drugs." It consists of strains of viruses and fungi that can be inserted into areas of opium poppy and coca plant farms that would kill all of the coca and opium."

"Isn't that a good thing to destroy the plants that produce cocaine and heroin?"

"It will also kill beneficial plants and wildlife and infect the rainforests where a lot of these drugs are grown. Colombia, for example, is not only known for growing t drugs, but it's also the home of rainforests that are called the "Lungs of the Earth" because they produce up to 20% of the world's oxygen for our atmosphere. This could have devastating consequences for life on earth as we know it."

"What have you decided to do with this classified report?"

"I haven't decided yet how to make it public. I don't want it to get into the wrong hands, but if we are a country that doesn't believe in weapons of mass destruction, then we shouldn't be developing them."

"Now that you have gone public with this information, what do you think is the solution?"

"I am calling for the U.S. Congress to conduct a special investigation into the safety of this technology. The FDA is not ensuring that it is safe for public consumption; the EPA is not ensuring that it is safe for the environment; and it's definitely not something that should be used as a weapon. It's my opinion that, at this stage, this technology is not safe for use as a food or a weapon of any kind, and that years of study should have been undertaken before releasing it to the public."

"Why was this technology released to the public?"

"Money. Germinat engineered corn, soy, and cotton that resist their own weed killers. They did it to sell more weed killer and to corner the market on that particular weed killer because their patent on it was expiring."

"You sound like an environmentalist."

"That's a label I never thought I would have. I thought I was just a traitor, a spy, and a whistle-blower."

"Whistle-blower, traitor, or just concerned citizen of the world? That is the question that is being asked around the world today about Seth Rogan who is perhaps the world's most wanted man. This is Pavel Kargin, reporting from *Russia Today*."

CHAPTER 4

Yuri helped Seth settle in to the safe house in Moscow. Tomorrow night he would take the nine-hour flight to the Far East. From the apartment, he could see the colorful and distinctive towers of St. Basil's Cathedral from his window and the glittering gold onion domes of the Church of Annunciation in the Kremlin. This was the Kremlin he had seen so many times on television. Back then, during the cold war, it had represented the seat of the Empire of Evil. Now it was oddly beautiful.

The American press was already doing damage control on Seth's report to *Russia Today*. The President called it "propaganda" and said that "The United States was against the manufacture of biological weapons." Spokesmen from the company said that Seth's report to RT should be disregarded as the words of a "traitor" and a "thief." Because of his fleeing the country, Seth's story was discredited in every mainstream media report.

"Okay, your name now is George Aimers," said Yuri, smiling, holding out documents. Here is new passport."

"I'm Canadian?"

"Yes."

"Does that mean I have to say 'eh' all the time?"

"Seth, Russians don't care what you say, but don't talk to people."

"Don't talk to people?"

"Don't go anywhere, just to work and back home."

"Sounds boring."

"Isn't that what you guys do in America anyway?"

"Well, yeah."

"Okay. Don't make friends. If you want girl, we get you girl."

"That sucks."

"Look, it's only for six months. Then you can do what you want. If you see anything suspicious, call me."

"Six months, eh?"

"Yes, six months. Oh, and shave mustache and color hair."

"What?"

"You prefer shave head and color mustache?"

"No, no, that's ok. I'll take the hair color."

"And we fix nose."

"What's wrong with my nose?"

"Nose too big."

"It's not."

"We fix anyway."

"Okay. Let me see if I've got it. Don't go anywhere, don't make friends, sleep with prostitutes that you send to me, and wear a disguise."

"Yes. You are smart. Don't forget to use lenses I gave you for eyes, and..."

"What?"

"Lose some weight."

Seth worked on his disguise with the materials Yuri had left in the safe house. He said a fond farewell to the mustache that had been with him since high school and picked a dark brown color to mask his light brown hair. With the contacts in, his eyes changed from green to brown. He didn't even recognize himself. The surface disguise was the easy part. Being George Aimers would be the true disguise to master.

CHAPTER 5

Seth sat in the covered balcony in his small apartment in the Far East that had been provided him and looked out through the dusty window at the frozen Russian landscape. The onset of winter was an amazingly beautiful contrast to the dingy, dusty look of fall. It started out rather beautifully, raining falling leaves of yellow, orange and red but then changed to a dusty, dead collection of sticks, and was followed by rainy, muddy streets littered with discarded bits of human invention. Winter was a much better look. The sun glistened on the glittery crystals of snow that covered every branch and every needle of every pine tree, which made the entire town look like a village in the middle of a Christmas forest.

Winston Churchill said Russia is a riddle, wrapped in a mystery, inside an enigma. That pretty much summed up the place. The young women were beautiful; the old women were hags. The people were highly educated, but most of them had lowly jobs. The summers were brutally hot and the winters stingingly cold. It was a country of constant contrast and vast inequality, but Seth found the people in the Far Eastern provinces to be warm and generous. If you knew when your last day of life was going to be, it was the best place to spend your last night on earth because, in Russia, people party like tomorrow will never come.

Seth had never thought he would have ended up here, so far from home, so out of touch with everything and everyone. He couldn't even use his own name. He was a man without a country, without an identity - traitor, a spy, banned forever from his own country, and all because he wanted to do something that he thought – no, knew – was right. Set things right. Like Einstein's great mistake, he had helped to unleash Armageddon on the world, and now he felt responsible to stop it.

Yes, the company had been good to him, had fulfilled his every material need, and he had reciprocated, but sometimes one man must fight for what he feels is right, even against the majority. Something that is wrong does not change to right just because the majority approves it, ignores it, or the government says it is right. It is still wrong.

He still saw the company and his country as being two separate and distinct entities. How had the lines blurred between the two, and where had he crossed over from loyal citizen to traitor? Had not the company betrayed his country and become the true traitor, and he merely the bearer of the news of that betrayal?

The Russians had been good to him. His choices were either Russia, Nicaragua or Venezuela. Not much of a choice, but Russia seemed the logical one for some reason. Initially, he thought, "Well, Moscow's not so bad or maybe St. Petersburg," but Yuri said, "Are you crazy? Do you know how hard it would be to keep you safe in a big place like Moscow?"

It was too close to the Western world, too accessible. Instead, Yuri pointed to a tiny place near the Chinese border in the Far East, about as far away as you could get.

"Khabarovsk? What am I gonna do there?" asked Seth.

"Stay alive. You'll be English teacher."

"An English teacher? I'm a scientist. We can hardly even speak English."

"Well, as I see it," said Yuri, "you have two choices - how do they say in cowboy movies - dead or alive? Anyway, look at bright side. We have some of the prettiest girls in world there."

"Great. Become a spy and meet women."

"You should have thought of consequences before you became spy."

"I'm not a spy."

"Just saying. Everything you do in this life has its consequences."

"Don't I know it?" Seth reflectively played back all the decisions he had made that set him on this path to such an uncertain destiny. This destiny had not been left to chance; it was a matter of choice, but the ultimate outcome was uncertain. He had been brave enough to do what he thought was right, which meant that he had to pay for that freedom of choice by accepting whatever consequences flowed from that decision. The effects of that decision would last a lifetime because destiny never closes its accounts.

"What's the big deal about these UFOs anyway?" asked Yuri.

"*GMOs*. Genetically modified organisms. You take one gene from one organism that has a trait you want and force it into the DNA of another organism to get the desired result."

"My uncle has pig farm. He's been doing that for years."

"No, this is different. You take a gene from, let's say, a fish, like we did with tomatoes, and you put it into the tomato DNA so the tomatoes can stand colder weather."

"Fishy tomatoes?" Yuri's face wrinkled with disgust.

"Or you take a gene from a bacteria that kills insects and put it into corn so, if the insects eat the corn, they die."

"Bacteria? Why you not die when you eat corn?"

"You don't die Yuri, not yet, you just get sick."

"These GMO - this is why Americans are fat?"

"Obesity, cancer, diabetes, digestive problems, allergies, attention deficit disorder, gluten intolerance, autism..."

"Okay, stop, stop. So, why you get involved with this GMO?"

"I thought it was a good technology that could be used to feed the world."

"We already have enough food to feed world."

"I know. I made a mistake."

"Like Einstein when he ask President to make atom bomb?"

"Yeah. Just like that."

As Gloria Steinem said, "The truth will set you free. But first, it will piss you off." In the process of learning the truth, Seth also learned how gullible he was. He was pissed off. Pissed off at Bill Penner, pissed off at Germinat, pissed off at the government, and pissed off at himself for being so stupid.

In his former life, he was Seth Rogan, graduate of Stanford University, considered one of the top genetic engineers in his field. Now he was George Aimers, the loveable English teacher from Vancouver. Well, at least he had been to Vancouver a couple of times and kind of knew what it was like, and it was true. There were a lot of pretty girls here in Russia. Seth worked at the local university. English was the only subject he could teach because his Russian was so poor. Russian had to be the most difficult language in the world with its masculine, feminine and neutral, and ridiculously infinite number of inflections. "How did the Russians even know what they were saying to each other?" Seth wondered.

For Seth, freedom now was a process. A process he had to fight for every day because every day someone was out there, waiting to grab him and take it away. He still had not had the chance to tell his story to the audience it was intended for – the American public. Whatever he said from Russia would be censored in the mainstream American press. What would get to any media outlets would be downplayed as coming from the mouth of a traitor and a spy. Seth had left America. He couldn't very well claim he was a good American citizen and wrap himself in the flag while he was, at the same time, hiding out in the enemy's backyard.

He was officially charged with violation of the Espionage Act, and he didn't expect he would have a chance to tell his story if he were caught. He would probably end up in Guantanamo Bay prison with the rest of the traitors and "terrorists" who are held without the right to counsel and without proper trials, and all because of the label assigned to them on their arrest. Seth couldn't count on the Constitution to protect him any more than he could expect his leather jacket to stop a bullet.

Yuri didn't understand what the "big deal" was about genetically modified foods or why Seth's own government wanted to kill him, but the stakes were high. Hundreds of millions of dollars had been spent on GMOs by the big chemical companies. They had decided that genetically engineered foods were the foods of the future. Those same chemical companies had inserted their top management into high offices of the United States government. They controlled the FDA. They controlled the USDA. In third world countries, government officials get bribes. In the states, they get job security with large corporations like Germinat.

The government knew the GMO food they allowed to be put on the tables of the American people was not safe, but they certified it as safe. Seth had irrefutable evidence of this in secret government reports. Not only that, he had in his possession a classified report that revealed this technology was being developed to be used as a powerful weapon. They could not let him live.

CHAPTER 6

Yuri picked up Seth and took him to a rundown boxing gym, which smelled like dirty socks. The wooden floors of the gym were covered with soft matting.

"What are we doing here?" Seth asked.

"Well, spy man, you need real spy training so you can survive out there. I'm gonna give you training," said Yuri, handing Seth an oversized and baggy jacket. Yuri himself was wearing the same kind of jacket. He looked like a worn out Michelin Man.

"Is that what these stupid jackets are for?"

"Exactly. This is Russian Sambo, best way to defend yourself without weapon. Put on jacket." Seth slipped it on.

"Anyone hits you, you hit back harder. Smart ones stay alive. Best to be prepared like Russian Pioneer. First thing I show you is back flip. Now, you come running at me like you are going to attack."

Seth ran at Yuri, and he easily flipped Seth over his back onto the mat and pinned his helpless body against the mat with his torso. Then he pushed down with his left hand on Seth's arm and raised his right fist within striking distance to his throat.

Yuri released his stronghold on Seth and stood up. "Get up," he commanded. "Now you flip me."

"What?"

"It's easy. I come running at you," said Yuri. "You take me by elbows and pull me to you. If you want, hold jacket at elbows and pull. Then bend right knee, crouch down and roll me over your back."

Yuri charged Seth, and Seth grabbed Yuri's elbows. "Now, bend right knee, crouch down, and roll me over your back."

Seth tried and tried but each time he was not able to incapacitate Yuri.

"This is no use, Yuri."

"Shut up. Never give up. Again!"

After much trial and error, Seth was able to flip Yuri. "Now pin me down." Seth did.

"Good!" said Yuri.

Seth practiced throwing Yuri over his back until he was good and sore.

"Now I show you front blocking. I come at you, and you take me by elbows, pull me into you, and trip me with leg." After practicing this a couple of times, they went back to repeat both exercises.

"Okay, now I show you how to get out of handcuffs and zip tie cuffs."

Yuri taught Seth how to fashion a makeshift key and pick the lock of handcuffs and made him practice with them both in front of and behind his back. He taught him how to break apart zip tie cuffs by centering the zip tie cuff lock between his hands and breaking the lock with a fast hit against his butt or his stomach, depending on whether he was tied in front or behind his back.

"Since you are such good student, now I show you how to defend against gun or knife. Now you put gun in my face."

Yuri handed Seth his gun. Yuri turned his head out of the way, and, at the same time, grabbed the barrel of the gun with one hand and struck the wrist holding the gun with the other, rotating the barrel and putting pressure against the trigger finger.

"Now you break finger," he said. "Then after snap finger, rotate upward, shift body, and throw him. Kick head and step here, take gun. Then shoot that fucking son of a bitch."

Yuri was a good teacher and insisted Seth meet him to practice self-defense and work out at least three times a week.

"You never know when you may need it," he said, "and you got nothing to do anyway."

CHAPTER 7

Seth had successfully installed himself into his new life in the Far East. It was cold most of the time but sunny. The people were very nice, but he couldn't communicate with them very well. It was just as Yuri said - go to work, go home, nothing before and nothing after. At home, he would work on his memoirs. Someday the entire story would be told... if he could stay alive until that day. Now he had to concentrate on being safe. For now, this monotonous routine was keeping him out of harm's way.

Seth wasn't hot on the idea of consorting with prostitutes so he made a compromise with Yuri and was actually able to meet some women (pre-screened, of course) using the excuse that he needed to work on his Russian language. Teaching his English class was not so difficult because the teacher's text pretty much outlined each day's lesson, and he had an "English only" policy in his class. As was the case with his high school Spanish teacher, nobody was allowed to express himself or herself in their native language, only the language of study. Since this was a university level course, and all his students had many years of English lessons, he could get away with it. Thankfully, nobody had asked him any questions yet about the English language that he could not answer or bullshit his way around.

Seth actually enjoyed discussing classic literature with his students. He assigned his favorites, like Steinbeck and Dickens, and never tired of answering questions about them but, when it came to grammar, he was completely incapable of explaining anything unless he read the explanation verbatim from the teacher's edition.

It was even more of a grind on the weekends. Yuri, his only friend, would check in with Seth every once in a while and bring him some English language DVDs from the local video store. English books were nowhere to be found, except the classic English literature from the university library, but Seth had a decent secure Internet connection and was able to download some e-books. It was like this, day in and day out, and the days sort of blended together. Then it happened.

It was before class on the first day of the week. The Director walked into the classroom with a beautiful girl. She was tall, with long, light brown hair tumbling around her shoulders and the most luscious, honey-sweet lips he had ever seen.

"Seth, this is Natalia," said the University Director. She's a recent graduate and will be your new teaching assistant."

Seth blanked out for a moment, finding himself staring at those luscious lips and her cherub rose cheeks.

"Oh, Natalia, I'm happy to meet you."

"Natasha."

"Natasha."

"Well, I'll leave the two of you now, said the Director. Seth ignored him.

"I didn't know I was getting a new assistant," said Seth.

"I didn't know I was going to be an assistant," she said. "I thought I was going to be an English teacher."

"Well, I'm not really an English teacher so..." Seth said, like a bumbling, nerdy, idiot scientist. He had to control himself.

"What?"

"What I meant was we can't always have our first choice, but maybe it leads to something better." *Finally an intelligent phrase,* thought Seth.

"I suppose you're right. Now where are you with the class?"

"Right to business, eh?" Seth had mastered the art of "eh" and took every opportunity to show off how Canadian he could be.

"Of course, we are in a university, not a nightclub."

"Yes, well..."

Seth wandered over to the desk, trying to be as suave as possible under the circumstances, picking up the textbook.

"Here is the text. We are about here..."

"Ah, form identical to infinitive used as a present subjunctive."

"Uh, yes."

Seth didn't know an infinitive from a subjunctive, but it was pretty easy to read the teacher's text and pretend to teach English. It wouldn't be so easy anymore with an expert looking over his shoulder.

"I have an idea," said Seth.

"What?"

"You want to be a teacher, right?"

"Well, it wasn't my first choice, but it is my profession."

"What was your degree in?"

"Philology."

To Seth that sounded like philosophy, but he didn't want to give in that he hadn't the slightest clue of what "philology" was so he just nodded in an understanding fashion.

"Right, well, what I was thinking 'aboat' (another Canadianism that Seth had mastered to perfection) was that you could teach the class, and I, as the master, could concentrate on some of the deeper subjects in English and maybe do some lectures and lead study groups on English literature."

"That sounds great."

"You have an American accent. How did you get that?"

"Oh, I lived in America for a few months - the work and travel program."

"Oh, really?"

"You're American, right?"

Oh shit, here comes the first lie. "No, actually I'm from Vancouver. People get us mixed up all the time."

"I see."

The class started to pile in and take their seats, regarding Natasha with passing curiosity. As the last student took her seat, Seth smiled at Natasha.

"Well, we'd better get to it," said Seth. "Class, this is Ms. "Andropova."

"Yes. Ms. Andropova is my new co-teacher, and she will be teaching the class today."

The process of meeting someone new, especially someone of the opposite sex, can be awkward, but it also can be rewarding. This meeting seemed to Seth to be the beginning of something nice.

CHAPTER 8

Seth enjoyed the company of his new assistant. Initially taken by her stunning appearance, he was now captivated by her personality. She was intelligent, had a wonderful sense of humor, and, despite their 24-year age difference, he was becoming quite absorbed with her. Usually, a girl was either pretty or nice. Natasha was both beautiful, and perhaps the nicest person he had ever met. Seth and Natasha started spending all of their off-time together. At coffee breaks and lunch breaks, there was never one without the other. It was like another world when Seth was with her, and that's the only world he wanted. Yuri was not as enthusiastic.

"No, out of question. Too dangerous," Yuri told him, furiously.

"Yuri, it's been four months already, and nobody has tried to kill me."

"Yet."

"I'm not asking you to break the rules, just bend them a little."

"So you can see girl? I told you, we have lots of girls. More girls than men in Russia. Every man can have two if he wants, or three. You want to have sex, I bring her here for you."

"It's not that."

"Oh, I see..."

"What do you see?"

"American spy is in love."

"Stop calling me that, and I'm not in love."

"Whatever you say, spy boy. Okay, I bend rules, but only little bit."

"A little bit doesn't count," said Seth, using a line from an old Russian song.

"I should never teach you Russian pop culture, wiseass. You can take her out, but where I decide, and I watch."

"Yuri, I didn't know you were a voyeur."

"You know what I mean, smart ass."

After a couple of weeks of "teaching" together, the ice between Seth and Natasha was completely broken. They spent all of their time away from work together - going out to dinner every night and meeting for coffee when they weren't going out to dinner. It was as if Natasha satisfied Seth's every need for companionship. When he was with her, he had no desire to be anywhere else or with anyone else. How strange that such a peace could overcome him in a land so different and so far away.

Natasha was mature beyond her 21 years. She had an "old soul." Because of the superior education system in Russia and the late blossoming of pop culture from the western world, which began trickling in freely during the 90s, it was like they had grown up in the same era. They had similar tastes in music, and both loved movies, which they watched in English at Seth's apartment. Occasionally, they watched a Russian film at the theater, which Natasha would translate in Seth's ear. Not only did it open the language for him, the tickle in his ear from her whispering was very pleasant.

The only bad part about it was that he couldn't share it with anyone. So many times he had been tempted to just reach out by phone, or even the Internet, to his parents or to his best friend in the states, but Yuri warned him that the U.S. government was listening in to all phone calls to and from the states and intercepting all emails from foreign locations to the United States, and Seth was a "hot potato." He could not risk revealing his location.

How was it possible, he thought, for the government to wade through so much data? Yuri said they looked for certain "key words," just like Google. Of course, anything associated with Seth would be a "key word." The government was hacking in to emails and Facebook accounts; nothing was private. They monitored and stored information from two billion phone calls and emails every day.

The Internet was a double-edged sword. It was the government's worst nightmare because of its freedom from regulation, but it made spying a lot easier. The U.S. thought nothing of spying on its own citizens. What was a little unconstitutional activity in advance of the public good? It allowed freedom of speech to run rampant on the Internet, not because it was guaranteed by the Constitution - plenty of constitutional freedoms had been modified, limited and curtailed - but because the government would rather have the people mouth off than let them exercise freedom of thought. Consequently, the Internet had turned into a huge gossip interchange. As Eleanor Roosevelt said, "Great minds discuss ideas. Average minds discuss events. Small minds discuss people.

Seth was completely cut off from the outside world. Even his Internet connection was so secure that it could not be used for communication. When he did research, he was isolated by a "Chinese wall" of electronic protections. He almost felt like he was being censored himself.

He never wanted this clandestine life - the secret life of a spy with no glamor. Everyone knew that the echelons of private industry in America were the ones who ran the government. It was obvious. The head of the SEC was the former head of the NASD. The heads of the USDA and the FDA were composed of ex-top executives from his ex-employer, Germinat Corporation, and that was no secret. In fact, his boss had been running back and forth between the government and Germinat for years - a recharging of evil, he supposed.

Science is a powerful thing, and powerful things come with responsibility. Manipulating genes and mixing species with other species had dangerous implications that required a responsibility to insure that no disastrous consequences result. Any change in the evolutionary chain of one species could affect the lives of hundreds, or even thousands, of others. This is a responsibility that Seth had never taken lightly, but, unfortunately, Germinat did. The bottom line is the company's only motivating factor for what it did or did not do.

It was no secret that genetically engineered foods were controversial, so controversial that his company and the other big chemical companies spent millions of dollars on PR campaigns to convince the public that GMOs were the promise to end world hunger and malnutrition. They would spend millions more to fight labeling to prevent Americans from knowing what they were eating, while their cronies at the USDA and FDA silently allowed genetically engineered foods to occupy up to 70% of the American table. Europe had already had its "coming out" when the only independent researcher was able to finally talk to the public about his findings on GMOs.

The dirtiest secret was that the entire process was flawed, and the flaws caused multiple repercussions that they knew about and probably thousands more repercussions that would not be discovered for years. Three billion years of evolution had forged a twisted, complicated path of genetics that mankind was only on the verge of discovering. Like once believing that the earth was flat and at the center of the universe, at the beginning of genetic engineering, we believed that each gene in a sequence of DNA was responsible for creating a single protein that produced a single certain trait, like blue eyes or fish that didn't freeze in freezing cold water. Little did we know that one gene could create proteins to produce many different traits. Instead of testing our theories, we forged right into production, forcing genes of one species into the DNA of plants, thinking they would create one desired effect, but the process of creating that one desired effect produced multiple effects we hadn't counted on. Those effects were deadly in many ways. The government knew how dangerous it was, and, not only did they let it happen, they certified it as safe. Seth was no longer happy to sit on the bench and be quiet. He had to be removed from the team.

CHAPTER 9

Confucius said "Choose a job you love, and you will never have to work a day in your life."

Four years ago, Seth was content. He had a great job. The pay was very good, he set his own hours, had no supervisor, and got to travel all over the world. The move from San Francisco to St. Louis took a little getting used to, but the boss had a cool setup in St. Tropez and every summer Seth stayed at the compound in his own little villa, right on the beach. With the parties at night on the boss' yacht or in town, the good life was an easy one to get used to and was a job that was too good to be true.

The Germinat bunch worked, played and lived pretty much together. As you moved up the ranks of this new world order, it wasn't important how smart you were. Sure, it had its place, but the most important thing was how loyal you were. Seth was a loyal employee, a team player. The hours were long, but the pay and the perks were great, and he had a lot of down time, as well as the opportunity to work on his own projects. Seth's friends were from the company, his girlfriends were from the company, and the guys who were married were married to girls from the company. The principal rule was "don't ever bite the hand that feeds you, and you will never be hungry." Seth should have listened to this one because the hand he bit would later bite back, and that bite had the full faith and credit of the United States government behind it.

Seth started out in this business as one of the "good guys." He was going to solve world hunger and malnutrition, but his company was primarily interested in preserving their monopoly on the world's best sold pesticide – Cleanup - before its patent expired in 2000. The first crops they engineered were crops merged with a soil bacteria that could resist glyphosate, the herbicide in "Cleanup." Their new patent for these "Cleanup Ready" crops would neither feed the world nor solve nutritional deficiencies in third world countries, instead, it would extend the protection of its patent, ensuring the sale of a lot of herbicide. "Cleanup Ready" crops were the backbone of the company's GMO products.

Seth was, however, working on a project he really believed in and was called "Miracle Rice." Miracle Rice was created by inserting a gene that produced beta carotene into a rice plant's DNA, which was hoped to solve one essential problem of malnutrition in young people in underdeveloped countries – vitamin A deficiency which caused blindness. The main problem was engineering enough beta carotene in the plant. As it stood, you would have to eat 20 pounds of Miracle Rice every day to get the minimum required amount of vitamin A, something that was better imparted by supplements or even carrots, but Seth vowed not to give up.

Bill Penner was Seth's boss. He was a VP, and you couldn't get much higher than that. Bill had an office that was as imposing as his ego and drove a very cool Ferrari in his off time. He was a tyrant so everyone at the company aspired to be on his good side. That was the key to a great promotion and, hence, a great life.

One afternoon Seth was returning from a lunch date with a very hot co-worker, and his secretary said, "Mr. Rogan, Mr. Penner would like to see you in his office right away."

This was his chance. Seth practically ran out of the room. The elevator couldn't move fast enough. He fidgeted around nervously while it slowly stopped at every floor on its way to the penthouse. Bill was more of an administrator than a scientist, but he also had impressive scientific credentials. He was somewhat of a social climbing, stuffed shirt, but Seth respected him and consid-

ered himself fortunate to be part of his team. He finally reached the penthouse floor, took a deep breath when the elevator doors opened, and then walked out at a quick pace.

The penthouse floor was all executive offices. It had an impressive conference room and even a private restaurant for the big wigs. Seth could get used to spending more time here. Bill's secretary showed him into the office. Bill was talking on the phone and seemed to ignore Seth at first, but when he saw him, he flapped his free hand in the direction of one of the two chairs in front of his massive, fine walnut desk for Seth to sit down. Seth sank down into one of the plush chairs.

"I know, Walter, but we've already been faced with this. You just need to follow the protocol, and everything will work out fine," Bill said into the phone. "Look, I've gotta go. Let's get together for lunch tomorrow and make a game plan, ok? Right-o, Walter, bye."

Bill hung up the phone and extended his hand to Seth. "Seth, how are you, man?" Seth stood up and completed the shake.

"I'm good Bill. You?"

"Couldn't be better. How's life treating you?"

"To tell you the truth, Bill, I love this job. Thank you. Of course, your St. Tropez hideout is an unexpected perk that I look forward to every year."

"That's why I picked you for a very special assignment, Seth, because you're a company man."

"Yes, I am. I'm very happy to be here."

"Seth, your credentials are very impressive. You're one of our only top-level biologists who is published."

"I guess I'm just a workaholic. Don't know what to do with all the extra time," said Seth.

"Yeah, well, we're gonna keep you pretty busy for the next couple months."

"How so?"

"Seth, we've chosen you to head a team to do a peer reviewed independent study on GMOs."

"Which GMOs, Bill?"

"Which? Well, we have a new corn that's coming out called Bt corn. We already know that it's safe for human consumption, but we need, you know, the test tube stuff."

For Bill, besides being more of an administrator than a scientist (his graduate training was a JD) he was even more of a politician. For him, the "test tube stuff" was a necessary evil.

"Take whoever you need. I want only the best on this team. We want to prove, once and for all, that our products are safe. This comes from the higher-ups."

"I thought you were one of them," said Seth. Bill laughed.

"But you did say independent study, right?" asked Seth.

"Yeah."

"How can it be independent if it's intracompany?"

"That's why we picked you Seth. You're published. You have the legitimacy that we need to counter crackpots like that old Scottish guy and his ridiculous claims."

"You mean Arpad Pusztai?"

"That's the guy."

"He's actually Hungarian."

Arpad Pusztai was a Hungarian biochemist out of the Rowett Research Institute in Scotland. He was one of the only scientists to come out against GMOs and was promptly discredited by peer reviewers. Seth had never read his reports, but he knew about them.

"*Whatever. The President called up Blair and told him to shut that mother fucker up. He was spouting all kinds of lies about our products.*"

"*The President? Of the United States?*"

"*Yeah. Look, what we want you to do is some independent testing on our Bt products and give us a full report so we can submit it to the EPA.*"

"*Not the FDA?*"

"*No, Seth, even though it's a food, the EPA is the one who approves it because it's technically a pesticide, and that's their bailiwick. You just have to evaluate that the Bt toxin in our corn is at an acceptable level for human consumption.*"

"*I'd be honored.*"

The EPA's jurisdiction over the corn seemed strange to Seth. How could a food be a pesticide? People eat food, not pesticides. The FDA's criteria for safety was a "reasonable certainty of no harm" from a proposed food. If a genetically engineered food were generally recognized as safe, if it had the same nutritional value as its non-GM counterpart, it was deemed safe for human consumption. With the exception of substances which were already known allergens that humans were susceptible to, testing was voluntary, and the FDA simply relied on the reports that the industry chose to give it. As a consequence, either GM corn, soy, and/or cotton oil or a combination of all those elements were in almost every packaged food in the United States, and everyone had already been eating them since 1994. In contrast, the EPA could allow foods with pesticides in them, as long as they were at "acceptable levels." Seth, as Bill said, was a "company man," so he accepted the job. How hard could it be? he thought. It's already been found to be safe. All Seth had to do was make some checks and balances. Child's play for an experienced genetic biologist like him.

"Great, now, like I said, you pick whoever you want. Your lab has a blank check."

Bill's phone rang, and he immediately turned to it, brushing Seth off. "I gotta take this, Seth, please keep me advised of your progress."

"Okay." Seth got up and turned toward the door.

"Oh, Seth," Bill called, putting one hand over the speaker of his phone.

"Yes?"

"We know the shit is safe. We just need more ammo. You know what I mean? Just get us what we need, okay, nothing more."

"Okay."

CHAPTER 10

Seth picked Robin Bender as his "right hand man" for the project. Robin was a respected botanist, and he would need a leader in the field for what he was being asked to do. Their first work was a test of Bt corn. Robin would be reverse engineering the corn, and Seth would test its effects on lab animals. Seth had never thought of Robin as a girl, although she was pretty attractive. Even in her lab coat, she walked with the sexy sway of a woman who was always ready to at least negotiate.

GM technology consisted of randomly inserting genetic fragments of DNA from one organism to another, usually from a different species. For example, the gene known to produce the Bt toxin is forcibly inserted into the DNA of corn randomly. Both the location of the transferred gene sequence in the corn DNA and the consequences of the insertion differ with each insertion. The plant cells that have taken up the inserted gene are then grown in a lab using tissue culture and/or nutrient medium that allows them to develop into plants that are used to grow GM food crops.

Bt corn was a form of corn that was genetically modified to produce its own toxin that would kill insects, primarily targeted at the European corn borer, an enemy of corn farmers. The same technology was used for cotton. The corn was engineered using a gene found in the soil bacteria, Bacillus thuringienis; thus, the name "Bt." When the gene was fused with the DNA of the corn, the corn actually made its "own insecticide." When insects ate any part of the corn plant, the toxic proteins produced by the Bt gene would penetrate the linings of their stomachs, and they would quickly die.

Seth and Robin had two control groups of rats. One was fed the Bt toxin itself in large doses. The other was fed the corn that produced its own Bt toxin.

Seth enjoyed working with Robin. Because of the pressure on them as a team, they both had assistants to do all the grunt work. Robin had brought her assistant, Shirley, from her department, and Seth had gone elsewhere in the company for his assistant, George. When 5 pm rolled around, Shirley and George ran out like they had heard the school bell ring. That left Robin and Seth, natural workaholics, spending quite a bit of time together.

The lab was not a romantic setting by any means. It was cold and stark, and resembled a science classroom in a university, but Seth and Robin often found themselves taking their work with them, and, as a consequence, spent many a dinner break together. Back at the lab, it was all work and no play.

"Robin, come here and look at this," Seth said, bent over his microscope. Robin was busy working on their next control group of GMO foods.

"Seth, I'm not the biologist."

"I know but look at this."

Still hunched over the microscope, and without looking up, he motioned for Robin to take a look. Robin came over to look, and Seth moved aside.

"Wow, is this the control group fed the Bt?" asked Robin not looking up.

"No, they're fine. This is the one we fed the corn."

"You're kidding."

"I'm not and look at this."

Seth spread a set of reports over the lab table.

"Look at the white blood cell counts. Look at this damage to the spleen."

"Seth, you'd better double- and triple-check this. I don't like the looks of this."

"I don't either."

The rats fed the pure Bt toxin were fine, even at high levels. The ones who ate the corn had smaller brains, smaller livers, and smaller testicles. They had irritation and structural changes in the cells of the stomach and intestines, and this was after only two weeks.

"This is looking very Jurassic Park," said Seth.

"I think it may be the process," said Robin pointing to her reports. "Look at these findings. The nutritional value of the corn should be the same, but it's 30% less."

"Something must be happening to the corn in the process of genetic engineering that was not expected," thought Seth.

It was always thought that bacterial genes were the best form of genes for genetic engineering. Bacterial genes were not as complicated as genes from most plants and animals because they did not have introns, which could create hundreds, or even thousands, of different proteins from a single gene, meaning that the gene could not only produce the desired trait but thousands of others so there was no chance that the bacterial gene could produce proteins other than the ones it was intended to create.

However, when the Bt gene was first introduced into plants, it produced very little Bt protein. To pump up production, they added introns because those increased Bt protein production. Instead of testing for whether the introns would also cause the production of other unintended proteins, scientists went with their original assumption that the gene would produce only the Bt protein and nothing else. They may have been mistaken.

    "I'd better talk to Bill."

CHAPTER 11

"You're gonna have to do better than shrunken rat's balls, Seth," said Bill, irritatingly.

"Bill, the rats have this after ten days. Imagine the cancers they could develop in six months."

"Rats get cancer from anything," said Bill. "They all get organ damage. I thought I told you how important this project was, and I told you that it has already been tested and found safe."

"You did. That's why I'm giving you my preliminary results."

"I want final results, Seth. Just get me a full report Seth, and don't fuck this up."

"I won't."

"I thought I was clear about this from the beginning. We just need independent data for our records."

"Right, but what about the government?"

"What about the government?"

"Don't they weigh in on safety?"

"Seth, you're a loyal employee to Germinat, right?"

"Right."

"You get a paycheck every two weeks, right?"

"Right."

"Well, so does the government. You get my drift? They work for us, not the other way around. We are the USDA, the FDA and the EPA."

"Okay. Got it."

"I hope you do."

"I do. I do."

"Great."

With a big toothy phony smile, Bill brushed Seth off. To Seth, politicians were a lot like toilets. They were all full of crap and when they got too full, they had to be flushed.

This was all unsettling for Seth who was the team leader because he didn't like what he was seeing. Being a relatively new technology, compared to the billions of years of evolution that had produced the plant, whatever was altered could have serious effects on the future of the plant life itself and anything in its ecosystem.

Everything in each ecosystem is interrelated. The process of evolution has created an intricate balance between the plant and animal life in the system. The plant, being immobile, depends on insects to pollinate it so they develop beautifully colored flowers and sweet nectar to attract the insects. The plant also needs to be able to distribute its seed so, through evolution, it developed a specialized seed distribution system. Surrounding the seeds with succulent fruits attracted animals who would ingest the fruit and express the seed by spitting it out, or the seeds would come out through their waste. This process has developed over millions of years, and now we come along and play God with it. God didn't need to create man to improve nature, and all that man had managed to do in the 200,000 years he has been here is to drive a mass extinction of species. Extinction of one to five species occurs naturally. Human activities were currently pushing extinctions at 1,000 to 10,000 times the normal rate.

These ecosystems aren't just pretty little forests that are fun to look at and play in; they provide essential services that we could not possibly perform for ourselves - like absorbing carbon emissions from human activity, thus having a cooling effect on the world's climate, decomposing tons of waste, returning it to the soil, providing oxygen for the atmosphere, filtering water, flood control, and producing food and fuel. Whatever Seth and the company did now could affect the environment for the next seven centuries, or even longer. Seven centuries was the short time that it took to rebuild a full rainforest.

It wasn't Seth's job to figure out the effects of GMOs on the ecosystem, only that they were safe for human consumption. Do the job, collect the check and benefits, and don't worry about anything else. Let someone else moralize about it. He could do that.

CHAPTER 12

Genetic engineering was messy. To force a sequence of foreign DNA into a plant, you couldn't just snip the desired gene from the bacteria and sew it onto the plant's DNA sequence like an old woman working on a quilt. The foreign intruder was loaded onto tiny shards of gold and shot with a "gene gun" into a dish of plant cells. This blasting created a lot of damage to most of the cells. The ones that "took" the foreign DNA were identified by an antibiotic-resistant, marker gene that is attached to the mix. The dish is doused with antibiotics, and the cells that emerge alive are the ones with the new form of DNA. This isn't the only way to identify whether the shot was successful, but it's the easiest one. One of the concerns that Seth naturally had was whether ingestion of the GMO foods could cause resistance to common antibiotics, but there was no way he could test for that in the time that he had been given. Another problem was that his test subjects were coming up with elements of neonicotinoid pesticides.

"Shirley, don't we have any samples of Bt corn that aren't contaminated? I'm getting conventional insecticide in the cells of my subjects."

Seth was visibly irritated.

"I'll ask for them, but I think they treat every seed."

"God damn it, how the hell can we test for anything when this shit is contaminated?"

"Seth, what's wrong?" asked Robin.

"What's wrong? This is a joke. We need corn that's not treated with neonicotinoids. Why the fuck do they spray them when they're supposed to create their own pesticides?"

"Because the Bt doesn't kill all of the bugs," said Robin as she ushered Seth into his office and closed the door behind them.

"God forbid if we don't kill all the bugs," Seth said, facetiously.

"Seth, you are always the first one to say it – there is no emotion allowed in the lab. It compromises impartiality."

"You really think this testing is impartial? You really think they care? It's a joke, Robin. They already have their fucking shit approved. This is a goddamned trap."

"Look, I'm sure everything is not as it appears."

"Exactly. Nothing is. That's the problem. I'm not going to verify a lie."

"Seth, I'm not sure I like where this is going."

"Robin, they douse the Bt stuff with neonicotinoids and the non-Bt stuff with Cleanup."

"I know. It makes it easier now for farmers to manage weeds."

"That just makes farmers use more glyphosate on their crops. We're supposed to be reducing dependence on pesticides, not using more."

"Seth, I need my job."

"Your job? That's all you care about?"

"Well, don't you?"

"Yes, but, take glyphosate for example."

"We're not supposed to test for glyphosate."

"I know, but we have to separate the effects of the Bt from a foreign competing toxin, right? That means we have to separate the effects of the neonicotinoid pesticides from the Bt. I'm just using glyphosate as an example because I know more about it than Bt. I wrote a paper on glyphosate. That's how the company noticed me. Look, the shit was originally proposed by the company as an anti-microbial agent."

"So?"

"That means they know it kills bacteria in the gut. I've seen studies linking it to cell death, birth defects, miscarriage, low sperm counts, DNA damage, kind of like the stuff I am seeing in my rats. A foreign substance like that could invalidate our entire study"

Seth's paper was about glyphosate's inhibition of CYP enzymes, which play crucial roles in biology; one of which is to detoxify harmful substances introduced through the diet that are not naturally present in the body. The study showed that glyphosate enhances the damaging effects of other foodborne chemical residues and environmental toxins. Negative impact is insidious and manifests slowly over time as inflammation damages cellular systems throughout the body.

"Glyphosate kills beneficial bacteria in the gut but not the bad ones, like Clostridium botulinum, Salmonella, and E. coli. The "good bacteria" in your digestive tract, such as protective microorganisms, bacillus and lactobacillus, are killed off."

"And..."

"That could damage the protective lining of the gut, allowing for toxins and bacteria to enter the bloodstream. This causes the body to send off an immune response to attack the wayward bacteria, potentially sparking autoimmune diseases. I'm seeing the same kind of stomach and intestinal damage in my rats."

"That means we either have to start all over again with seeds that aren't treated or try to isolate the effects of the neonicotinoids to eliminate them from the equation."

"Which is impossible."

Germinat was treating every GM seed, even the Bt ones, with neonicotinoid pesticide. When the seed grew into a seedling, the *toxin passed throughout every cell of the plant through its vascular system. It was all through the plant, at levels that were so high Seth vowed, after this experiment, never to eat GMOs again. The toxin was embedded in the plant. You couldn't wash it off.*

CHAPTER 13

Seth was actually getting used to his adopted Russian home, especially now that he had somewhat of a social life... if you could call it that. Khabarovsk was a nice looking town and was by no means a tiny village. It was a real city with restaurants, nightclubs, and a beautiful downtown area. The golden domes of the churches glistened during the day, and the Disneyesque, beautifully sculptured ice city in the main square was particularly alluring at night when it was colorfully lighted. All the traditional Russian stereotypes that Seth expected were missing.

His apartment was not much to look at from the outside. In fact, it resembled old tenement housing or perhaps even a bomb shelter because of the lack of homeowners' associations, but inside it was quite comfortable and had all the modern conveniences, and it was never cold. Central heating worked during the cold months, and you didn't even need to wear a long-sleeved shirt inside because it was so warm. Quite a contrast to the states where, if you got up in the middle of the night to go to the bathroom, your feet met an icy, cold floor, followed by chilly air. Russia was much warmer – well, inside it was warm. .

The warmth also extended to his new social life. Spending time with Natasha made the time go faster. Everything was fun. They went out together practically every night, but, of course, Yuri was always lurking in the shadows somewhere. Seth thought that was kind of creepy, but, when he was with Natasha, he forgot completely about Yuri. At some time, and he was not quite sure when, she had become an important part of his new life, and he couldn't imagine it without her.

"George, why do you always carry that briefcase around with you?" Natasha asked one evening at dinner.

"I don't know. It's just habit, I guess. Plus, my mom gave it to me, and it makes me feel close to home when I have it."

"You should get it fixed."

"What?"

Of course, she was speaking about the bullet hole in the leather. It looked like someone had stabbed it with a screwdriver or something. It was true that Seth always had his briefcase with him, and he supposed that was drawing some sort of suspicion. He took it every day to class, and, whenever he went out with Natasha, he also took it with him. In fact, since that day he was clutching it on the plane, he had never let it out of his sight.

"When are you going back home?"

"Oh, I don't know. I still have to finish out my contract at the school."

"Yes, but aren't you going to visit during the holidays, maybe?"

"I don't know. We'll see."

"Tell me what you would do during the holidays when you lived in Canada."

"Well, I had a friend with a villa on the beach in St. Tropez so I used to go there quite often."

"Wow, he must be really rich."

"Yes, he's a rich and important man... has a yacht too. It was a great place – always a lot of fun. The South of France is amazing. It just feels good there. It's sunny, the people are nice, and there are a lot of cool places to hang out."

"Like where?"

"Well, they have restaurants right on the beach. You order a local fish that you could swear they just caught for you. It was so fresh, and the waiters would come to your table and put on a show to prepare it. At night, the whole town of St. Tropez turns into a party, and you just kind of walk around and enjoy it."

"Sounds great. I actually went to France right after I graduated from the university."

"Really? Where did you go?"

"A friend and I took a tour to Spain, France and Italy. We spent about a week in Paris that was fantastic."

"I used to live there."

"Really? Paris?"

"Yeah, in my college days."

"Do you speak French?

"Mais oui, bien sur."

It was actually one of the reasons the Russians had decided to make him a fake Canadian, not that many of them speak French in Vancouver.

"How did you like Paris?" he asked her.

"I loved it. I love the architecture and the art. There's always something going on."

"Yeah, it's kind of like a Disneyland for the adults." Natasha laughed.

"I used to go to the butcher or the fish market and pick out what I wanted for dinner and then over to the wine store to get the perfect matching bottle of wine," he said. Natasha giggled. "Then next door to the bakery for a nice dessert if I were having company over, and, of course, to the fromagerie for the perfect after dinner cheese."

"What a production, and just for dinner! You probably had a better one at home than we have here in this restaurant."

"That's Paris. Everything is always first class, always proper. Everything has its own place and its own silverware. For example, did you know that we are eating our cheesecake with fish knives?"

"What?" she said, looking surprised.

Seth held up the silverware they had been given with their dessert. The small, pretty but oddly shaped knives had little notches in the top, and they had matching forks.

"We have fish forks too."

"That's hilarious. I guess they don't know what they are here, but they looked fancy so they gave them to us for our dessert," she said.

"Why not? The dessert is fancy," said Seth. Natasha giggled.

"I'm sure in Moscow they would not do the same."

"No?"

"No way. Moscow is very sophisticated."

"I heard it was one of the richest cities in the world. Everything seemed quite expensive when I was there."

"Everything is expensive there. Someday we have to go there and eat the fish with our dessert knives."

That had Seth bursting out laughing, and, like catching a yawn, Natasha chimed in to the point where people around them were staring. Like a line, the shortest distance between two people is a laugh. Seth and Natasha were closing all distances between them at great speed, getting closer and closer to each other. Seth was falling, through space and time, in love with Natasha, and he hoped to fall deep enough to stay there forever.

CHAPTER 14

Yuri was hanging around Seth's apartment again. Seth had no reason to complain because, as limited as his social life was, it was good to have someone he could call a friend, but tonight he was expecting Natasha and had to get rid of Yuri.

"Yuri, Natasha's coming over tonight."

"You gonna get lucky tonight?"

"Is that all you think about?"

"Well, did you fuck her yet?"

"Yuri...just because she's a woman does that mean I have to fuck her to enjoy her company?"

"Well, yeah. I don't know. I don't think I ever enjoyed the company of any woman without fucking her."

"Well, I do. For now, she satisfies my every need."

"How can she satisfy your every need if you don't fuck her?"

"When it happens, it will happen. Until then, I'm not going to obsess about it."

"Whatever, but what you should obsess about is to stop calling attention to yourself," said Yuri.

"I'm the foreigner. I don't have to call attention to myself. It comes naturally."

Foreigners are kind of like freaks. They look funny, talk funny, and always seem out of place. Seth constantly felt like the odd man out everywhere he went.

"Well, if you want to continue to have such freedom, don't abuse it."

"Sorry, I won't."

"And stop taking that fucking briefcase everywhere. It looks suspicious. You did turn over all reports, didn't you?"

"Of course, I did."

"Good, because, if you held out on them at all, they will not be as friendly as Americans are to you."

"You think the Americans have been friendly with me?"

"Well, you pissed off some very important people, Seth. That can be expected."

"At least, I'm not in the news anymore. Thank God. What horseshit they dreamed up to say about me - that I stole sensitive government secrets. I guess that's what happens when your boss leaves the company and becomes one of the most powerful men in the world."

Bill Penner had been appointed head of the FDA by the President, and Robin's boss, Ted Peters, was appointed to head the EPA, not bad for a company whose mainstays were pesticides and genetically engineered seeds. Germinat had been quietly buying up all the seed companies in the world since the late 80s. Their aim was to control the world's food supply. The seed supply business alone was a $32 billion per year enterprise, but the pesticide business was even better, predicted to reach $65 billion per year by 2017.

"Look," said Yuri. "I know you think I'm some kind of super spy, but I can't be around to protect you all the time. Just always watch out. It only takes two seconds for someone to come up and put a bullet in your head."

"I'll be careful, but I still have to live."

"Exactly. If you want to *live*, do like I say."

"Okay, Mr. Super Spy."

"Very funny. You don't have to kick me out because I have to go now anyway. I will be watching," said Yuri as he walked toward the door, reaching for his coat and hat and slipping into his boots.

"You'll be watching. That's really a fine idea to have in my head for romance."

"I didn't mean I will be watching you have sex."

"I hope not. Take care."

"You too, public enemy number one," said Yuri.

Seth chuckled. What else could he do? Seth did qualify as public enemy number one, especially since the U.S. was not being run by the public anymore. They didn't even know what they were eating, and he had become the bad guy, all because he was trying to warn them. As Yuri was opening the door to leave, Natasha was just arriving.

"Ah, George, look, beautiful girl is here." Yuri smiled from ear to ear at Natasha. "Privet."

"Privet."

"Okay, kids, don't get into any trouble. Papa is watching," Yuri quipped.

"Good night, Yuri," said Seth.

"Do svidanya," said Natasha, as she unbuttoned her coat and placed her hat on the hat rack while kicking off her shoes. Seth closed the door and latched it.

"Who is that guy Yuri? He's always hanging around," she asked.

"He's a spy."

"No, seriously."

"He's just a friend. Just another guy who speaks English."

"I guess you need your practice."

"Of course, I am an English teacher after all."

"He just seems so unlike you. So unsophisticated."

"Well, everybody is different. And I don't have the chance to make very many friends here."

"That's true."

Natasha and Seth sat down on the couch. "Can I get you something?" he asked.

"No, I'm good," said Natasha, pulling some DVDs out of her purse. "I got us some movies to watch."

"Oh, cool. Now we need something to snack on while we watch."

"Popcorn?"

"No, too American. I'm Canadian, remember? How about wine and cheese?"

"Sounds great." Natasha started to get up, but Seth beat her to it.

"I'll get it. You put in the DVD and figure out how to set it to English," Seth said, going into the kitchen for the cheese.

"You don't know?"

"I'm impatient."

"You never told me whether you have a girlfriend back home."

"Not really a girlfriend. It's over anyway," Seth said, returning with the cheese. "She was just someone at the company where I worked."

"What happened?"

"She married her boss."

"Really, and he was also your boss?"

"No, we had different bosses. She was from a different department."

"Yeah, what did she teach?"

"Botany."

"Sounds boring. Was she pretty?"

"Yes, of course. That's a pre-requisite," he said. Natasha smiled.

"I see, but you never got married?"

"Never fell in love. Not really. I thought I was once, but it was just infatuation. That intense feeling that feels so good at its peak, and then you realize that there's nothing else to it."

"That's nothing to base a marriage on."

"Nope, they say that getting married for sex is like buying an airline for the peanuts." Seth laughed and Natasha caught the laugh.

"You always laugh at your own jokes?"

"Only when they're funny."

That started another pleasant dose of cortisol and endorphins.

They settled in, drank wine, watched the movie, and Natasha cuddled up to Seth. It felt good. After the movie was over, she stayed close to him, and Seth finally made his move. Actually, it came quite naturally. He stroked her hair as she rested her head on his shoulder. When she moved to look at him, he took her face gently in his hands and kissed her on the forehead, cheeks, and then on the mouth, tasting her tender lips as they parted to receive him. The sensation was an explosion of feelings, leaving in its place a pleasured memory of that moment. That, thought Seth, was pure heaven.

CHAPTER 15

After only two months, the rats that had been fed the GM soy in the second controlled experiment started showing signs of infertility. There were sets of male rats who were sterile, and the females that did produce offspring produced smaller-sized rats.

Seth and Robin were on their usual dinner break, just kicking back, and, of course the conversation turned to work. What else did either of them have in their lives? They had been sipping on wine for the whole meal and were both getting a little tipsy.

"Now I'm getting blue testicles instead of pink," said Seth. "Bill's really gonna love this."

"I can hear him now," Robin said, mimicking Bill. "Seth, it's gonna take a lot more than your blue balls to convince me of anything."

Suddenly, they both started laughing uncontrollably. The neighboring couple scowled at them, and they toned it down to snickering.

"Well, you must have them, right?" she asked.

"What?"

"Blue balls."

"I don't have blue balls."

"Well, I don't see any girls around."

"I have girls around, and I have you. Speaking of that, don't you have a life at home?" said Seth.

"You're just asking me now?" Robin asked, annoyed. "How long have we been doing this Seth, two months? Don't you think if I had a boyfriend, he'd be wondering why I was hanging out with you every night and getting home at two in the morning? What would you expect him to think? That I'm a vampire?"

"*Yeah, I guess so.*"

"*You guess so?*" Robin laughed. "*You men are really unbelievable.*"

"*Yeah, I suppose we are.*" Seth looked around, and saw that the restaurant had cleared out. "*What time is it?*"

"*Shit. It's midnight already. I'm surprised they haven't kicked us out of here.*"

"*I'd better take you home.*"

"*You trying to take advantage of me?*"

"*Maybe.*"

The thought of it had actually crossed Seth's mind, and more than once. Robin had nice, green eyes and, without the lab wear, she was even sexier, and she always smelled good. Seth was surprised she hadn't been taken by now. Of course, she was always working, and he was the only man there. Cock block works every time. Seth had been so hard at work, he had forgotten he was so horny. He had always been horny, and now he was shocked to come to the realization that he had actually forgotten.

They paid the check, and Seth offered his arm to Robin, walking her to his car. They had left hers in the company parking lot.

Seth could see that the alcohol had more than lowered Robin's inhibitions. She was deliberately flirting with him. Normally, charming and innocent, when she got into the car, she slowly slinked in and glanced at Seth with inciting eyes that must have just seen their awakening. The way she looked at him, like he was a piece of candy that she wanted to put in her mouth, made him so nervous he almost lost control of the car, swerving off to the shoulder.

"*Whoa, cowboy, watch it,*" she said as Seth swerved back into the center of the lane.

"You just made me kind of nervous, that's all."

"Well, do you like what you see?" Robin smiled and playfully tinkered with the fringe of her dress, exposing some of her bare leg.

"Yes, I do."

"Didn't you ever notice before?"

"I did."

"But what?" Robin giggled. This was definitely an invitation and not one to be refused.

"Just waiting for the right time."

"And that would be..."

"How about right now?"

"Here?"

"If you want."

"Slow down. Why don't you just take me home, and we'll talk about it there?"

"Okay." Seth could feel his heart beating faster and, well, other things tingling too.

Robin's apartment was clean and cozy. Unlike the apartment of a scientist, more like an artist's place. She had collected little knick knacks from her travels and, of course, she had plants, lots of plants. There were green, leafy plants, ferns, and flowering plants all over, and her balcony was a rose garden. She also had a collection of orchids, Seth's favorite flower. Robin entered the living room with a drink in each hand, the ice gently tinkling like little wind chimes.

"You like orchids?" she asked, handing him his drink, then she sat down next to him closely.

"Love them."

"What do they remind you of?"

"Well, they're very feminine."

"You're very observant. You know, orchids are delicate and need special care, just like all feminine things."

"I know all about orchids, and feminine things."

Seth took his cue and reached over to stroke her hair, gently pulling her face closer to his. Their lips met with a tender and powerful force. At that point, they melted into each other, and Seth felt a flush of sensations over his entire being. Hands wandered naturally, and each caress became more exciting and pleasurable. Where the body ended and the soul began was a mystery in this ancient game of combinations.

CHAPTER 16

Back at the lab, Seth and Robin switched back to their "working relationship."

Robin was bent over her microscope, examining slides from a sample of Bt soy.

"Seth, I don't get this," said Robin.

"What is it?"

"Well, there is supposed to be just one gene in this soybean plant, along with the Cauliflower Mosaic Virus promoter, of course."

"Yeah, that CaMV virus thing always freaks me out."

"Well, that viral gene has to be there, or the plant can't produce the proteins from the engineered gene."

A genetic sequence from the Cauliflower Mosaic Virus (similar to the HIV virus in humans) was the "promoter" that was used in every GMO food, whether it be the gene for artificial insecticide or the herbicide resistant gene, to "turn on" the gene so it would produce the proteins that gave the desired effect. This was discovered by independent researchers in Europe in 1993 after GMOs had already been approved by the European Food Safety Authority, and it caused a big controversy. Why? Because Germinat didn't tell the regulators of the existence of the viral gene. They were unaware of it when they approved the genetically engineered foods.

Bacteria and viruses were the materials of choice in engineering GMOs because they are natural cell invaders, and that, after all, is what genetic engineering is all about – forcing something into a cell that didn't belong there naturally. The researchers in Europe were concerned about the safety of the viral gene because

73

it produced several proteins instead of just one, each protein having its own function or trait. One shut off the plant's ability to protect itself from viruses. Another produced random proteins in cells, the effect of which nobody would know for years or maybe even centuries. Another suppressed the plant's anti-pathogen defenses, making it unable to naturally defend itself and making it highly susceptible to certain pathogens. The researchers concluded that the viral gene promoter was a toxin, leading to the question of whether it would express itself in the food products made from the plants.

"Seth, are you dreaming? I said look at this." Robin seemed both surprised and upset.

Seth shook himself from his thoughts and looked at the slide.

"What am I looking at?"

"That's just it. See those two other DNA fragments?"

"Yeah. I do."

There were two foreign gene fragments unrelated to the cleanup gene or the natural genes in the soybean plant.

"How do you think they got there?"

"It could be that the DNA was scrambled when they inserted the gene, or..."

"Or what?"

"Or the soybean's own DNA could have rearranged the sequence to try to correct the errors in its DNA. Jurassic Park again – nature finding a way, and this DNA strand is large enough to produce its own protein. This could be the reason we are seeing tumors develop in the rats."

Seth's neck was aching from bending over the scope. When he straightened up to rub it, he saw his lab assistant, George, looking

right at him in a strange way, like Seth had caught him mastur-
bating.

"George, do you need something?"

"Uh, no."

"Did you run those sequences I asked you to yet?"

"Uh, not yet."

"Okay man, get to it. I need those."

"Okay Seth. Sorry." George trotted off to comply with the re-
quest.

"It's alright, George." Seth turned back to Robin. "We have to
figure out what's going on here. I'll try to get in touch with those
guys from Europe and discuss their findings."

"Okay," said Robin. "I'll move on to the other studies."

"Yeah, it's crunch time. Let me have a report on this finding
before you leave tonight."

"I thought we were going out tonight?"

"Oh, shit. I'm sorry. We are... just got a lot on my mind."

"I know. Me too." George and Shirley, of course, left at 5:00
p.m. on the nose. Time slipping away the way it does, it was 8:00
p.m. before they knew it.

"We'd better go before they shut down every restaurant in
town," said Seth. The small cities in the outer reaches of St. Louis,
Missouri rolled up the sidewalks at 10:00 p.m.

It had been a while since Seth had a real girlfriend, and it was
nice to be around Robin. Dating had always been an annoying
aspect of life. It was more like a series of job interviews than shop-
ping. If it lasted after four dates ("Sex and the City" rules) that
meant the girl was not considered a "slut" if you had sex with her,
but it usually never went far enough for him to find out if the sex
were going to be really good or just a "relief pitch." Consequent-

ly, when he reached a point with a girl where the sex was pretty good, that's when the relationship ended, and most of Seth's relationships were based on the sexual aspect so, of course, they disintegrated. If you're not looking for the right thing, you can't be disappointed if you don't get it.

CHAPTER 17

"We fed these rats 500 times the amount of Bt that the corn produces, and there's no damage to their tissues. This group ate the Bt corn, and I've already had eight out of 40 die with organ and tissue damage on the others, and that's with the clean seeds," Seth said to George.

"Tests prove the Bt toxin is destroyed by the stomach before it gets to the intestines," retorted George.

"I looked at those tests. They're test tube tests, using hydrochloric acid and pepsin to simulate digestive fluids, but the rats are showing erratic cell growth in the lower part of the small intestine. That's the last point before getting into the colon."

That meant either the testing was flawed, and the Bt was surviving the digestive process, or, even worse, the unpredictable DNA sequence that was created in the process of genetic engineering was creating a toxic protein that damaged the cells in the rats that ate the corn. Seth's rats had lesions on their stomachs and abnormal and accelerated cell growth in the lower part of their small intestines.

"I definitely need to talk to Bill about this," said Seth. "Where did George go?" he asked Robin.

"I don't know," said Robin, "Maybe he went to the bathroom."

George had disappeared again, as he tended to do whenever he was needed. It seemed that, after every frustrating event in the testing process, George was nowhere to be found. It was like he was running out to tattle tale on Seth and Robin.

"He must have a weak bladder," said Seth. "He's too young to have a prostate problem."

When Seth and Robin got back to the lab after dinner, the door was ajar. Seth looked closer and saw that it had been broken open.

"Robin, call security and stay back," said Seth, nervously.

"What's wrong?"

"Someone has broken into the lab."

Seth ventured into the lab itself. It was a mess. Equipment was smashed. Chemicals were spilled all over the floors and tables. Their colors mixed together like a first grade class had been finger painting on the floor. Lab beakers and flasks were smashed, laid out in pieces like some crude mosaic. File cabinets had been ripped open and their contents spilled out. Seth quickly sat down at his computer and logged in. It had been hacked. The hard drive had been taken. He turned to yell for Robin, and, just as he did, he saw a man in a ski mask, raising his arm above Seth's head. Less than a second later, he felt a thump against his head, the lights went out, and Seth fell to the floor like a lifeless bag of potatoes.

When he came to on the ambulance gurney, Seth was looking through a tunnel with an assortment of blurry, upside down faces at the end of it. Two EMTs began to roll him out of the lab, and he noticed that, not only were Jess and Tim, the night guards there, but so were two members of the local police, writing reports, asking questions.

"He's awake," said Jess, walking along with the gurney. "Seth, hold on buddy, they're taking you to the hospital."

"Wait. I don't need an ambulance. I'm fine." The EMTs stopped rolling him for a second.

Bill Penner was also there. "Seth, when you're done with the doctors and the police, and, if you're up to it, we need to talk," he said.

"Bill. What the hell happened here?"

"Someone trashed the lab," said Bill. "Probably vandals."

"We've had these a couple of times. They're usually looking for drugs or stuff to make meth," said Jess.

"Yeah, but we always catch 'em," said Tim. "But these guys were good."

"How?" said Bill.

"They don't show up on the security tape... at all."

The company had one of the most sophisticated security systems in the world. Whoever did it was able to bypass that system and enter the building undetected.

"I don't see how they could have snuck in without us seeing them," said Jess. "Unless..."

"Unless what?" said Seth.

"Unless they were already in the building."

"That's just not possible," said Bill.

"Not only that," said Seth. They took the hard drives... and the slides. Everything."

"The lab animals are all dead," said Jess.

"Don't let anyone touch them. They need to be autopsied," said Seth. "Put them in the refrigerator, now," said Seth.

"Can't do that," said Jess.

"Why not?"

"They're all hacked up. Can't tell which is which. Looks like the floor of a sausage factory."

"Looks like vandalism," said the police detective. "We're just about done here. Should be okay to clean up in the morning."

CHAPTER 18

Seth's eyes fluttered, the hammer still pounding against his head. He felt dizzy and sick. He sat up in the hospital bed, his head spinning, then swung his legs over the side of the bed. He had to get out of the hospital and get back to the lab, which was in pieces. Luckily, he had kept a copy of not only his own, but also Robin's reports on a duplicate hard drive, and he had duplicate copies of all their slides and physical data at home. Something had told him in the very beginning of this project that it was going to be the most unusual one he had ever undertaken, and, for that, different precautions had to be taken.

The fact that the computer hard drives had been taken was proof that these were not thieves looking for drugs. Was it industrial espionage from a competitor? They were out to either steal or destroy their data but why? That was something he had to find out, as well as put together the broken pieces of their experiments and finish the job.

Seth walked into Bill's office about 10:00 a.m. the next day, his head still pounding like a pile driver.

"Seth, what are you doing here, man? You should be at the hospital or home or..."

"It's okay Bill, I'm fine. I need to finish this job."

"Seth, forget about it. This job is fucked. I already put Audrey Stevens and her team on an independent study."

"No, Bill, I've got everything."

Bill flashed a look like a patient who was getting a rectal examination.

"What?"

"I saved copies of everything - all our data, every slide. All we need is to clean up the lab, and we can take up where we left off. Of course, we've lost our control groups. That sets us back time-wise."

It was like Bill was choking on something, but then he quickly recovered.

"Smart man. That's great."

He patted Seth on the back, and Seth winced.

"Uh, sorry. We'll get you back to work right away."

"Great, Bill. I just need Robin."

"Seth, Robin asked to be reassigned."

"What?" said Seth in consternation.

"She was very specific. Also said that she didn't want you to try to contact her. I think this break-in really scared her."

That was a surprise for Seth. Now he was the deer in the headlights. Seth and Robin had worked together, played together, eaten together and slept together the past four months, and now she wanted to get out? Why so suddenly, and why did she want to get out of everything, including the experiments? This was not right. There had to be more. Then again, when emotions were involved, a woman didn't really need a reason for anything, at least no reason that any man could understand.

"Alright, Bill. I'll pick a new team member. I'll get this job done."

"Atta boy," said Bill, and dove for his phone.

Seth got back to his wrecked lab and office and immediately dialed Robin.

"Yes, Seth?"

"What's happening?"

"I don't know what you mean."

"I mean, Bill said you were out of the project."

"That's right."

"Why?"

There was a pause, so silent that the only thing that could be heard was the static on the phone and footsteps in the corridor.

"Robin?"

"Seth, it's over. Please don't call me anymore."

"Robin, we're not in the tenth grade."

"I mean it Seth, don't call me and don't try to see me. If you do, I'll consider it harassment."

Then Seth heard the click of the phone being hung up. In that one click, Robin was no longer a part of his life, and he had no idea why. Seth knew it wasn't a serious relationship, yet there was a sadness in the realization that it was over, and so suddenly. It was as if every memory of every breakup suddenly melded into one. By now, times should have changed, his shell should be thicker, and a wealth of experience should make this more bearable, but he felt teenage rejection overcoming him like a childhood virus that lies dormant, then attacks the unsuspecting adult. It would never be something he would get used to feeling.

CHAPTER 19

Long days go quickly but take their toll. Seth was exhausted after putting the lab back together. At the risk of breaking in an entirely new team, he let George and Shirley both go back to their regular jobs and set about the task of going over the resumes of Robin's replacement.

Seth had rebuilt the lab, and the extra security surveillance video equipment he had ordered had been delivered and installed. Everything was ready, except that he needed to select a new assistant. Seth poured over the stack of resumes on his desk. The person had to be qualified but not too much of a company person, like Robin, and it had to be a man this time.

After a while, he found himself reading the same sentence in the same resume, over and over again. His brain was unable to process any more information. That was his cue to go home.

Seth's memory took over on autopilot, guiding him to his parking space while he went over all of the latest events in his mind. He could not assume that vandals broke into and destroyed the lab. He had taken precautions to guard the data. He had made multiple copies of the data on disc, multiple copies of all the reports, and split up the duplicate copies of the slides. Instead of leaving his working copy at the lab, he would take it with him wherever he went. The only thing left to do was to think of a place to hide the duplicate copies.

Seth arrived home, parked his car, and shuffled into his apartment. His mom had given him a beautiful briefcase when he graduated from Stanford, but he never used it because nobody used briefcases anymore. Everyone carried laptop cases now. He took the briefcase from its special place in the closet, dusted it off, and put all of the duplicate data and hard drives in it.

The next day Seth went in late to work because he stopped by the bank. He withdrew $30,000 in cash from his savings account and put it in the briefcase, as well as his passport... just in case. He had, unknowingly, created a go-bag. He rented a private, safety deposit box at a different bank and put the go-bag into it. Hopefully, he would never have to use it.

CHAPTER 20

It was lonelier at the lab without Robin. Seth's new partner, Daniel Harkavy, had the charm of a dry piece of toast, and he wasn't much fun to look at either, but he was intelligent, diligent, and seemed to have Seth's scientific sense of duty.

"Dan, did you go over the tests on our ratty friends?"

"Yes, no signs of mis-folded proteins. What we are seeing, though, is Bt toxin in the blood cells, intestinal walls, spleen, liver, and even feces."

"Lemme see that. What levels?"

"270 ppm." 270 was considered toxic.

Seth knew this meant that the Bt made by the GM plant was transferring to bacteria in the digestive system. This was not good. The control group, fed higher levels of the naturally occurring Bt, had no such symptoms... at all. This had to be a different kind of bacteria. Something in the genetic engineering process had turned it into a deadlier toxin.

Seth went into his office, recorded the findings, and sent them by secure email to a duplicate web mail address under an assumed name. Then he made two flash drive copies, one for the experiment and one for the go-bag, which he put in a hidden compartment in his jacket. Seth was beginning to feel like James Bond. Too bad there was no Q at the company to set him up with a cool car and weapons to defend himself from the bad guys.

At 11:00 p.m., Seth left the office. He would go by the bank the next morning on the way to work and stock up the go-bag. He headed straight home. Gliding into his parking space, Seth looked up and noticed the light was on in his apartment. He didn't think he had left it on, but he had done it several times so it wasn't really unusual, but he was overly nervous from the break-in.

Seth observed for a while. He must have left the light on this morning. He was being paranoid. Take a deep breath and go, he said to himself, as he remembered a line from an insurance claim that Johnny Carson had once shared on "The Tonight Show" – "I glanced at my mother-in-law and headed over the embankment."

When Seth came to the top of the stairs, everything looked in order. The door to his apartment was closed. He tried to open it quietly. It was locked. That was a good sign. He unlocked the door and slowly inched his way into the apartment, like he had seen in detective movies. The only difference was that detectives always had a gun.

Slightly slinking half of his body into the apartment, he was suddenly pulled in like a fly into a vacuum cleaner and struck on the head. The curtain was down on Act II.

When Seth came to, he was face down on the floor eating dust. He sat up, and a shiver went up his spine in his panic as he frisked himself, finding the secret compartment in his jacket. The flash drive was still there. He straightened out his stiff body to stand up, and, as he did, his head throbbed. His right arm felt heavy and weak, like his hand had been super glued to a shot put. His knee ached from hitting the floor. The apartment looked even worse than he did. The living room floor was a collage of papers. The refrigerator had been purged of its contents and it had been strewn all over his kitchen floor, like fish out of water on top of a goopy paste that looked like some kind of GMO Pepto Bismol. Seth picked up some ice from the floor to put on his head. Then he dialed 911. When the operator answered, "911 emergency," Seth thought, "Wait a minute. If this were the company, I can't talk about anything being missing."

"I made a mistake," Seth responded, and hung up.

He would go back to the lab tomorrow, like nothing had happened, and continue with the testing, using the duplicate data. Seth went to his home computer, but, of course, the hard drive was missing. What a surprise.

Carefully checking every hiding place was a must, not only to make sure the predators had left, but also to see if they had, in fact, found everything. Finding the aspirin was easy because the contents of his entire medicine cabinet had been emptied into the sink. His bed had been torn apart and the contents of his drawers, as well as the drawers themselves, carpeted the floor of his bedroom. His clothes had been ripped out of the closet and were in a jumbled pile on the floor. Where the bed should have been was just the frame. The mattress was against the wall and looked like Lizzy Borden had taken turns with Lorena Bobbitt on it.

At least, there was no need to move the bed. Seth pushed aside the clutter, exposing the rug, and shoved that to the side. The floorboards looked intact. He went into the kitchen to fetch a knife from the kitchen floor and limped back to the bedroom. Prying open the secret compartment in the floorboard, he found that it was all there – his spare MacBook with the duplicate data on it and his father's 357 Magnum. He remembered when his father had given it to him.

"Son, they called the Colt 45 the Peacemaker. I like to call this little gem the Insurance Adjuster. If you use it right, you will make your life insurance company proud. I hope you never have to use it."

Seth slipped the Magnum into his belt and went to the remnants of his living room to power up the MacBook and make a copy of the flash drive. He was smart, but he had to be smarter. No points for second place.

CHAPTER 21

Bill was, of course, on the phone when Seth was shown into his office. Bill flashed the usual fake smile, and nosed Seth to sit down. After what seemed like an eternity of blah, blah, blah, he finally hung up.

"Seth, how are you doing?" Another shake and a smile.

"Everything's coming along Bill." Bill looked stoic.

"That's great," he said. "Uh - when can I expect your report?"

"Just going through and analyzing all the data. Shouldn't be too much longer."

If Bill knew anything about the break-ins, it wasn't showing,, but politicians were famous for double-speak and were consummate liars. That's why George W. Bush had to be their favorite President. It's easier to commit a fraud when the actor believes his lie to the point of a conviction.

"Seth, take your time. Team 2 has already turned in their report."

Team 2 was pretty quick. It must be easier to work without getting whacked on the head every time you try to save your data.

"Okay, Bill."

On his way back to the lab, Seth's mind drifted to a thought that kept gnawing in the corner of his brain – the ecosystem. Everything in life was interconnected, from the smallest insect to the tallest tree, but nobody cared about the ecosystem. Nature was doing a good job thousands and even millions of years before GMOs but he wondered, "If the Bt that was killing the rats were that strong, what effects could it have on life in the ecosystem when the GMO plant pollinates?" The results could be disastrous, from pollinator deaths to human respiratory problems, allergies, skin lesions contamination, extinction of other plants, and God knows how many species that depended on them?

The ultimate plan was for the company to own all the seeds and to engineer the GMOs to be sterile so all seeds had to be purchased from the company. The current plants were still capable of reproduction, and the company had to take the alternative step of suing farmers who saved their seeds with patent violations. Since the GMOs were not sterile, that meant they could breed with natural varieties of corn, soy, and cotton and contaminate them and, finally, insect pests were very adaptable to changes in their environment and could easily develop resistance to the Bt toxin, resulting in crop failure anyway.

The U.S. official policy was to bring GMOs to market as soon as possible for the benefit of mankind, of course. Oftentimes, what was seen to benefit mankind was destructive to nature, without which mankind could not exist. As Albert Einstein observed, human beings experience thoughts and feelings as something separated from the rest, a kind of optical delusion of consciousness. We forget that we humans are animals, inextricably connected to the world and everything in it. In the rush to bring GMO food to the world because it was good for us, nobody had asked the question whether it would be good for the world.

CHAPTER 22

Strangely, Seth was almost fully assimilated into his life as an English professor in Russia. He didn't miss his moustache at all. He rather liked the clean-shaven look. Sometimes when he looked in the mirror, he didn't even recognize himself. If Seth had to spend the rest of his life here, he thought that he could, and it may happen.

Unfortunately, he was obliged to stay in town and was not able to leave so his sphere was somewhat limited. When Natasha invited him to the country with her friends, he was tempted to break that vow he had made to Yuri.

"Come on. It will be fun," she said.

Fun – what an interesting concept. Seth's clock had been set on survival so long that he didn't realize he was starving himself of an essential element of being, that of having fun.

"I don't know. I really don't know anybody."

"That's okay. You'll be with me."

That was convincing. The chance to spend the entire weekend with Natasha was as compelling to Seth as a porch light to an insect. After all, he was no longer Seth Rogan, the American fugitive; he was George Aimers, the Canadian English teacher. What could possibly go wrong?

"Okay, I'll go."

"Great! We'll come by your place Friday around 8 to pick you up."

That was good. Yuri would have already made his obligatory visit and would have made plans to go out and get shit-faced and party. Seth had already made it clear to him that his partying days were over, and he could count him out. Yuri left Seth alone for the most part on the weekends so, once he was able to sneak away, all he would have to do is answer his phone if Yuri should call.

When 8:00 p.m. rolled around, Seth felt like a kid sneaking out of his parents' house. Natasha's friend, Masha, and her boyfriend with the rhyming name, Pasha, drove them.

"All the girls are bringing their boyfriends," said Natasha.

"Oh, does that mean I'm your boyfriend?" he asked. Natasha smiled shyly.

"I'll take that as a yes."

On the way to the country, the world outside the jeep looked frozen and cold, but it was warm inside, and Seth had his Russian winter provisions for outside - a good pair of boots, a fur hat and coat, and fur lined gloves. There was no room for *People for the Ethical Treatment of Animals* in Russia. If you didn't wear fur, you froze so you wore fur.

They pulled in to a compound with high security - no passport, no passage, and your name had to be on the list. The place was a camp for employees of the Russian Central Bank. It had a sauna, a swimming pool, and several recreation rooms. When they arrived, Masha and Natasha joined the other girls in the kitchen, and Pasha scurried Seth out into the great outdoors with the men to barbeque shashliki, a delicious Russian marinated meat. Just as they didn't believe in suspending the fur trade, Russians were not vegetarians either.

The cold was biting at his tingling fingers through the gloves and his ears through the hat so Seth warmed his hands near the open barbeque, which was pouring out a delicious smelling combination of smoke and steam. The guys were all gathered around doing the same thing and drinking beer. Pasha tried to translate for Seth while he turned the meat with one hand and held a bottle of beer with the other.

"George, you're from Canada?"

"Yeah."

"What kind of a car do you drive back in Canada?"

"A Lexus."

The guys all reacted in chorus. A Lexus was definitely something they all would love to have.

As they feasted inside, it seemed like every man had a toast for their newfound Canadian friend. Seth couldn't decide if the toast were a reason for drinking or the drinking a reason for talking, and he decided it was the latter. Alcohol is a kind of truth serum. Without it, you may doubt sincerity. With it, you can doubt sincerely.

"Seth, how long have we known each other?" Pasha asked rhetorically, looking at his watch. "I'll tell you - four hours and nine minutes, and, in those four hours and nine minutes, I have seen only goodness in you. I want to say that I'm happy to call you my friend and invite you to my home, anytime you want. To you."

As Pasha raised his glass, eleven other glasses met each other at different levels in the middle of the large table, followed by a practically synchronized swallow, a joint exhalation, and the sound of twelve glasses hitting the table almost simultaneously. Seth discovered that night he had two extra stomachs - one for vodka and one for overeating.

Then one of the guys pulled out a guitar and started playing. As members of the group joyfully sang old Russian folk songs, some of the girls began to dance. Seth didn't know any of the lyrics, of course, but chimed into the chorus phonetically.

After the last bottle was emptied, the girls cleared the table while the guys went off to play billiards and table tennis. Seth surprised himself again to find that he could actually play with competence two games that he had always thought he played badly. When the girls were finished with their tasks, the guys all followed them to the pool area for a sauna and swim.

Seth sweated beads of vodka in the sauna room while making small talk with the guys. When he could stand it no longer, he made his way to the pool. Spotting Natasha, he jumped in and swam underwater to her like a shark, pulling her underwater by the legs.

"You're drunk," she said, as they surfaced.

"Not any more. I sweated every drop of vodka out."

Seth held Natasha and spun her in the water, then leaned in for a kiss. She promptly pulled away and swam off with Seth in pursuit.

Being with Natasha, set Seth at ease, so much so he forgot what even brought him to Russia in the first place. As their weekend was coming to a close, for the first time, he did not have a care in the world.

CHAPTER 23

The pleasant weekend had quickly come to an end. As the car pulled out of the compound, everyone was in a jovial mood. If this had been America, there would be no way that jeep could have navigated the ice-packed, snowy roads, but Pasha skillfully slipped and slid along like a professional driver who had driven icy roads every day of his life. Everything was great, until they got to a police checkpoint near the river.

The police motioned for Pasha to pull over, and he did. Then, they looked inside the jeep, and that is when things went from bad to worse.

"Dokumenti, pajaoulasta," said the officer to Seth, asking for his documents with an outstretched hand.

Natasha quickly chimed in, speaking Russian, asking why, as Seth was a passenger, not the driver. It was no use to argue. Seth complied, giving his passport, and the officer took it into the police station, leaving Seth and his friends in the car.

There is a fine line between police and criminals, which makes it a better idea to play by their rules than to argue with them. Arguing with a man who has the same emotions, fears, and pressures that we all do, but who also can deprive you of your freedom is never a good idea. There is no such thing as freedom of speech when you are dealing with a policeman.

Seth took the opportunity to call Yuri. Yuri's voice was like an electric shock.

"You what? I told you not to leave the city!"

"I know Yuri, but could we talk about that part later? I'm getting a little nervous here."

"Damn right you should be. What if they arrest you and take your fingerprints? What then, smart guy? Don't you know you are most wanted man in world right now? I make call."

Yuri angrily hung up and the police returned, but with more questions, not the passport. Now they had his registration, with his address, his immigration card, and his passport. If anyone wanted to run surveillance on English speaking white men from North America living in Russia, now they had a nice lead.

Relativity should have been about the perception of time, because it has a strange knack for running out when you need more of it, and lasting too long when you want it to pass quickly. Seth sat in the car and waited for what seemed like an hour. Finally, he was invited to come inside, and Natasha tagged along with him as his interpreter.

The policeman turned them over to another policeman who had Seth's documents and a ticket book and form.

"He said your registration is not up to date," said Natasha.

"That's impossible. It's for the whole year. I haven't even been here a year yet."

"Well, that's what he said."

"Ask him how we can solve this," said Seth.

The solution turned out to be putting 1,000 rubles between the pages of the ticket book. Seth had back his passport, his registration, his immigration card, and a valuable lesson; fugitives don't leave the hideout.

CHAPTER 24

"Seth, you really fucked up this time," said Yuri. "This means no more privileges, no more restaurants, no more coffee shops. You go to work, and you go home."

"Really, Yuri, there was no harm done."

"You don't know that. I'm sure they are looking for anyone who could pass as American. There are a lot of guys like that in Moscow, but here? You're a dead giveaway."

By putting Seth at the ends of the earth, Yuri was trying to get him farther out of harm's way but may have done the opposite.

"For how long? I can't really live like this."

"But you *will* live."

Yuri chewed on his bottom lip, as if to stimulate his brain to thought. "Let's give it some time, and, if there is no heat, you can do your coffee shops but don't ever leave town again."

The next several weeks were excruciatingly boring. Seth had to confine his time with Natasha to the university grounds, and he couldn't explain why. He hoped it would not be devastating to their fledgling relationship. Seth looked upon his boredom as an opportunity – the time that he would not have otherwise had to do everything he never seemed to have the time to do. In this time, he worked on his memoirs. Someday his entire story would be told, and it was important to nail down his exact story.

One day, strange as it may seem, another Canadian showed up at the university, claiming to be on a sabbatical. Worse yet, he was a scientist. Seth tried to stay as far away from the man as he could, but, after a faculty meeting, the inevitable happened, and it was Natasha who introduced them. As he left class one day, Seth found himself trapped in the corridor, nose-to-nose with Natasha and the new Canadian.

"George, this is Dave Salisbury, our new biology professor and guess where he's from?"

"I can't guess. Where?"

"Vancouver! Isn't that great?"

Fucking wonderful, thought Seth. He didn't know shit about Vancouver except that it was cold and rained a lot, and it was not far from Seattle.

"George is from Vancouver too!"

"Oh really?" said the newcomer. "What's your alma mater?"

"Ya know, I'd love to sit with you and chat, but Natasha and I were working on a lesson plan, and we have to get to it. Sorry, eh?"

"Sure, no worries. Maybe the two of you would like to get together with my wife and me for dinner or something?"

Natasha chimed in, "That would be great!" at the same time as Seth's "We'll see," and he whisked Natasha away.

"Why did you react that way? He's from Canada too."

"I don't know. Just seems kind of fishy."

"Fishy? Why?"

"Well, think about it. We are a zillion miles away from North America, and the only other guy who speaks native English is also from Vancouver? Doesn't that seem fishy to you?"

"Well, yes, but I'm sure it's just a coincidence. You don't have any reason not to socialize with him so..."

Seth had every reason not to socialize with this guy and a great deal to hide, not to mention the fact that he couldn't answer one question correctly about Vancouver. He didn't even know if they had a baseball team. He had better read up on Vancouver and learn to change the subject every time it came up.

"Let's get together with them. It will be fun," she said.

Seth was not sure he could handle that kind of "fun," but it was true. He was becoming stir crazy in his new situation of "house arrest."

"Okay, I'll think about it."

Natasha hugged him around the neck and kissed his cheek. Seth would have to hit the Internet and brush up on Vancouver.

CHAPTER 25

The curtailment of Seth's social life felt like a big step backward, and Natasha didn't understand why Seth was turning down her invitations. After two weeks of isolation, Seth came to the realization that something had to be done, or she would interpret the restrictions as rejection.

Seth decided to venture out of the apartment a little bit at a time. It was the Camel's Nose principle. If Seth snuck out a little bit longer every time, he would soon have his freedom back, or, at least, that was the theory. A "double date" with Dave and his wife was the perfect excuse to slip his nose under the tent.

"No way. It's too early," said Yuri.

"Look, this guy is from Vancouver, supposedly so am I, and there's nothing between us but a sea of Russians. If I don't accept his invitation, he's going to think something is up."

"You're right. He probably will."

"So?"

"Go ahead and accept. I am going to check this guy out."

The double date was for Friday night at a nice Armenian restaurant. Seth was actually looking forward to it until Yuri rang the bell Thursday night.

"He's FBI," said Yuri.

"Who?"

"The guy from Vancouver, and you don't have to worry. He's not really from Vancouver or Canadian either. His real name is Brian Jenkins."

"What does he want? He has no authority over me, does he?"

"They obviously suspect who you may be, and it's probably from that fucking police stop, but no, he has nothing over you. Except, of course..."

"What?"

"If he wanted to shoot you, but that would more likely be CIA."

"That's reassuring."

"Well, if they knew where you were, they would just shoot you, and you would never suspect it."

"Oh, thanks Yuri, I feel much more comfortable now."

"Don't mention it. Next time listen to what I tell you. Now we have to listen to this guy and figure out what the hell he's doing here."

"How do we do that?"

"I'm coming with you."

"Bringing a hooker to our double date?"

"Who said anything about hooker? I bring my own girl."

"You have one?"

"No, but this is Russia. I get one; it's easy. You study about Vancouver and think of some questions this guy won't be able to answer. It will be fun."

Yeah, great fun. The party was expanding. First Seth, the spy by no choice of his own, then Yuri, the FSB agent, and now the FBI. It was becoming a real alphabet soup of international espionage.

CHAPTER 26

The Bt toxin that was produced by the bacteria and the one pro-
duced by the corn plant were completely different in toxicity. Seth
could not explain why, but the rats who ingested the regular Bt
had no effects at all. However, the ones that ingested the Bt corn
had multiple effects - such as infertility, shrunken testicles, organ
damage - and Seth and Daniel found evidence of the Bt toxin
breaching the digestive system and in the blood of subjects. They
also found elevated antibodies and an increase in cytokines. There
was no way this corn was fit for human consumption. Tissue sam-
ples from the ileum, the lower part of the small intestine, showed a
significant increase in cell growth. This meant possible precancer-
ous activity.

"Dan, if this corn hits the market, there's going to be the risk
of allergic reactions, autoimmune diseases, birth defects, and in-
fertility... not to mention cancer."

"I've checked and rechecked the data. They definitely have to
go back to the drawing board on this one," said Dan.

"What about the pollen?" asked Seth.

"Tests conclusively deadly to butterflies and possible endan-
germent to bees."

"That means anywhere within a one- to two-mile radius of
where this stuff is planted, pollinators are going to die. That could
affect the whole ecosystem."

"We're also showing nutritional content is less in the Bt corn
than comparable conventional corn."

Seth knew that these problems may be irreversible and that it
may be many, many years before the full negative effects were re-
vealed. It was difficult to postulate what effects resulted from the

neonicotinoids, if any, and what effects were from the Bt toxin, but Seth theorized that, since the toxin was found in high levels in the areas with abnormal cell growth, it was the primary culprit.

Seth's tenure at the company had been preceded by a report he had done on the effects of glyphosate. The levels of glyphosate in non-organic vegetables and animal feed had skyrocketed since the advent of Cleanup Ready crops. Since glyphosate was the active ingredient in the world's most popular herbicide, and its patent had run out in the year 2000, the company had genetically engineered corn, soybeans, and cotton to be resistant to its glyphosate-based product, Cleanup. Seth became an expert on the poison and its effects on mammals for the study, and he now surmised that the company may have hired him just to shut him up.

Glyphosate had even far more devastating effects than the neonicotinoids alone because it was an anti-microbial agent. Essentially, it killed off the good bacteria in your digestive system, leaving the bad bacteria like E. coli to wreak havoc, contributing to diseases like "leaky gut." Seth's recruiter at the company had promised Seth he would work on a team that would make improvements in the products to avoid glyphosate exposure. Of course, this never happened, but Seth was equally sold on the Miracle Rice project and really believed in it.

The after effects of glyphosate had already seen its effects on the general population. More and more people were becoming sensitive to certain components of foods and developing allergies that had never been seen. Gluten intolerance had become so prevalent that gluten free items were being advertised. The rBGH hormone, genetically engineered by the company to make cows produce more milk, had also sprouted conditions like intolerance to lactose.

The pieces were adding up. So many chemicals were being introduced into the food supply that approximately 70% of all processed foods were made with either high fructose corn syrup, cottonseed oil, canola oil, or beet sugar, all of which were genetically engineered company products. Seth was finally in a position where he could try to convince the company not to put another hazardous product on the market. Consequently, he was meticulous in his analysis of the data and the preparation of his report.

"Bill is not going to like our report," said Dan.

"It is what it is."

Seth spent the better part of the next day preparing the report, complete with all the backup and details of each test result. The finished product was a fine example of his best work ever. It was finally ready for Bill.

Bill's face as he read the report looked like he was enduring the smell of a lingering fart. Finally, he looked up from the report in seething disgust.

"Seth, I thought I was clear about this."

"You were. You told me to do an 'independent study' and that's what I did. I can't help it that the corn is poisonous. It is what it is."

"No, Seth, it is not what it is. Your data is faulty."

"Faulty? No, my data is solid."

"Your experiments were interrupted by the break-in. They're not conclusive."

"Bill, I have all the data, and all the findings. It's all there."

"Still I have to go with Team 2's report. They conclusively have proven that the Bt toxin does not survive digestion."

"In test tubes with simulated stomach acid."

"Yes."

"*Well, then how do you explain these tissue samples and the Bt toxin in the blood of the rats, breaching the placenta to offspring and ending up in the brains of the offspring?*"

"*Seth, we're tabling this research. It's inconclusive. I'm going with Team 2. Thanks for your help, but the decision has been made.*"

"*Bill, this corn cannot go to market. It's too dangerous.*"

"*God damn it Seth, don't you remember what I fucking told you the first day? This is an independent study. The corn is already approved. It's already in everything you eat, every day - every can of soda, every cookie, every cracker, everything. You have as much chance of stopping this train as you would of finding balls on a Brahma Bull.*"

The corn was already on the market. How could the company have let that happen? Seth's stomach turned. He felt a lump in his throat. Kids were eating this stuff, all over America. It would only be a matter of time before there were increased allergies, birth defects, cancers, infertility, and nobody would know where the blame really lies.

"*Bill, we have to do something. I know we can make a safer corn. I know we can.*"

"*Bt corn, soy, cotton - it's all approved. That train has left the station, Seth. Our reports show that it's safe. That's how it got approved. Team 2 says it's safe. The only one who says it's not safe is you. They mostly feed this shit to cows and pigs anyway and make ethanol out of it.*"

"*Bill, you have to...*"

"*I don't have to do anything. That's it, Seth. I wish I could thank you for this report, but I can't. It's being tabled as non-conclusive. That'll be all Seth.*"

Seth began walking out of Bill's office as Bill called to him.

"Do I have all the data in every format?"

"Yes." Seth was lying.

"No copies were made? All the slides and results have been turned in?"

"Yes."

Another lie. Seth had always prided himself on his integrity. Telling the truth had been the hallmark of that pride. Now, lies were becoming an everyday occurrence in his life and that tugged at his self-esteem, but he thought to himself, "Sometimes lies can get you into trouble, but if you really want to get screwed, try telling the truth all the time." He was now in the possession of something so dangerous he didn't know what to do with it - dangerous to his job, dangerous to himself, dangerous to the company, and potentially dangerous to the government. At this point in time, Seth wished he could be someone else. He wished he could close his eyes, tap his heels together and say "there's no place like home," and vanish.

CHAPTER 27

As Seth was leaving Bill's office, Richard Roberts, the wiry Assistant Administrator for the Office of Chemical Safety of the EPA was walking in. Seth wondered why the EPA would be making a house call. Bill could provide him with Team 2's report, an independent study on the safety of Bt corn, at the same time he was shredding evidence that the corn was a deadly toxin.

As Seth went to bed that night, he couldn't sleep. Every time he tried to close his eyes and drift off to sleep he imagined deformed babies and hairless kids on chemotherapy. Bt corn may be a killer, but this job was going to kill Seth before the box of Cheerios and rBGH milk did.

If Seth went to the press with what he had now and tried to blow the whistle on Germinat, the best he could do was lose his job and insure that he would never work again in any capacity in his profession. He needed something more.

To fight his insomnia, Seth tried taking walks to clear his head, but it only stimulated him to think of ideas on how to get his hands on more evidence, which kept him awake. There was only one way to find it, if there was any. He had to break into Bill's office and hack into his computer.

Seth was used to keeping long hours so it would be easy to have access to Bill's office. He knew he would be able to hack into Bill's PC once he got in. All he needed to do was figure out a way to break-in.

At home, Seth used the extra key from his office to make a bump key. All the locks at Germinat were the same model. Seth's bump key would go into the lock on the door of Bill's office and, after a few taps of a screwdriver, Seth would be in. The next question was when to do it.

Seth lay in bed, night after night, unable to sleep. Once he blew the whistle on Germinat, what next? Would he be hailed as a hero? Take to the talk show circuit? Write a book? One thing was for certain. The company was going to fight back. Seth would be discredited, blacklisted in the scientific community. If blowing the whistle had no immediate economic reward for Seth, he would be lucky to get a job flipping GMO hamburgers and pumping GMO cola at McDonald's. He definitely had to weigh the pros and cons on this one. There were many cons - no company car, no more trips to St. Tropez, no cushy perks, no more conferences with hot and cold running blondes. The pros, only one, if someone would actually listen, he may be able to save lives, human and animal, and, the bigger picture – the environment; something the EPA was supposed to do instead of helping the company poison the world.

Germinat was buying up seed companies. It also bought Beescience, the research company that was trying to solve the problem of poisoning of the pollinators. Germinat's herbicide, Cleanup, was the most popular brand in the world and, thanks to Cleanup Ready GMO corn, soy, and cotton, the three most common components of processed food and animal feed could be sprayed with even more Cleanup. It would kill everything but the crop itself. Too bad for the monarch butterfly that depended on the milkweed, once flourishing in the wild and which now grew in between the crops. Cleanup was so good at killing that it killed every form of plant life, except of course, the Cleanup Ready crops.

The company would own every seed company, and every seed would be genetically engineered, and the patent owned by the company. It would become the master of the U.S. and then the world's food supply. An essential part of monopoly is elimination of democracy. To do this, the company stuffed the coffers of Congressmen and Senators' campaign funds. The ignorance of the voting public was an advantage for the company that sewed its political crops as much as its genetically engineered ones. Germinat and other huge companies and banks, which were really just a collection of greedy people feeding ultimately on the public, had succeeded in forming a government around their interests.

Seth went back to work on Miracle Rice, the company's biggest hype project and the one that he had once believed in. Funny thing about a belief - no matter what seemed to point in the other direction - there was nothing that could talk you out of it. The brain carefully selected facts to rationalize and reinforce your belief, and ignored everything else, no matter how logical. The Bt corn testing gave Seth pause to look at what the company was doing with Miracle Rice and all of its products.

Besides Miracle Rice, the company's paradigm shift in the world's food supply by replacing natural foods with GMOs was making a product that allowed it to sell more of its Cleanup herbicide and making a product that produced its own pesticide. How that fit into the company's plan to increase yields, feed the hungry, and reduce pesticide use was anyone's guess.

The business of agriculture was a big business. The company sought to control the food supply. As long as it could genetically engineer a food with any type of nutrient, it didn't matter that the world diet would only consist of rice, corn, and soybean fed pork and beef. Land would continue to be cleared of native plants, the overuse of pesticides and monoculture crops would strip the soil of its nutrients and poison it for generations to come, but it wouldn't kill the company's crops. If the company could make rice with beta carotene, who would need carrots? The world could be fed by the giant industry of processed foods, being pushed by cartoon characters on children who would pester their parents to buy Sponge Bob happy meals and Dora chips. As the pollinators died out, if you wanted fruits or nuts, all you had to do was pay more for the imports. Besides, who needed fruits and nuts, unless, of course, it was M&M's chocolate covered peanuts with artificial chocolate flavoring, of course, because, without the pollinators, there could be no chocolate either. There was a chemical solution to all of America's food needs which had been whittled away for years and years and honed down with precision to train the public that everything they needed to put on the table for their family came in a box, bottle, or can.

Genetically modified foods were a grab bag of pesticides, allergens, toxins, dormant viruses, and antibiotic resistant molecules that were being consumed by humans for the first time. It was only a matter of time before their immune systems became unable to recognize what to protect against. In this experiment, the entire American public were the test rats and the chemical companies the only winners.

CHAPTER 28

Seth kept a close eye on Bill's office every afternoon after he left, waiting for his opportunity. During his surveillance of Bill's office, he had observed Richard Roberts there on at least two occasions. Roberts was a lanky gray-haired nerd with coke bottle glasses, which Seth supposed he had constantly removed for ass kissing and brown nosing. The coziness of company officials and the EPA and FDA was nothing new. When they were not working for the company, they were both working at the EPA or the FDA. When they were not working for the EPA or FDA, they had a place at the company. It was called the "revolving door," and neither Washington nor the company made any attempt to conceal it. The many meetings that Roberts had with Bill didn't look right, especially in light of the report Seth had just turned in on Bt corn.

The timing of the break-in had to line up fortuitously so Seth had to be prepared to move on a moment's notice. The best time was after most of the personnel had left and only the die-hard workaholics like Seth remained at their respective posts. Seth had spent enough time at the company after hours to know the schedules of the maintenance people and knew each one by name. They would not suspect anything if they saw him wandering the corridors to get a caffeine fix or use the restroom.

Insomnia from 1:00 a.m. to 6:00 a.m., fatigue from 9 to 5, and anxiety thereafter became a routine for Seth during the following two weeks. Then, when it seemed that he would never have an opportunity, all of the ducks lined up in a row. Bill had left at the usual time between 5 and 6, the cleaning crew had left early, and Seth found himself almost alone with enough time to break into Bill's office, hack his computer, check his files, and leave at about his normal 10 to 11 p.m., without arousing the suspicion of security.

Of course, Seth had neither made nor used a bump key before, nor had he hacked a computer so he had practiced on his apartment lock with a bump key, which worked famously, and practiced changing passwords on his own PC at home. If crime were your career choice, the Internet had a play-by-play explanation of how to break, enter, and hack into computers, among any other criminal skills you could imagine. There were even YouTube videos on the subject that you could play and follow along.

Carefully, Seth maneuvered his way toward Bill's office in the general direction of the coffee machine with his coffee cup in hand – the one with the company logo. As he approached the door of Bill's office, he could feel his heart pounding in his chest and the pulse in his neck. With the anxiety, his heart rate had increased to at least 130 bpm, which is what you would expect on a nice jog, and he was hardly moving.

Seth looked up and down the corridor and, seeing nobody, got out his bump key and screwdriver. He inserted the bump key, a perfect fit, as it had been on his own office door. Then he tapped with the screwdriver and turned the key, only to find resistance. The bump key was not turning the lock. "Shit, after all this, the fucking thing doesn't work," he thought, as he wiggled the bump key in the lock, while, at the same time looking up and down the corridor, as if he were crossing a busy street and trying to check his cell phone at the same time. Another tap, tap with the screwdriver and nothing. Then Seth heard footsteps in the corridor, aborted the mission, and headed to the coffee machine.

What had gone wrong? The bump key had worked on his own office door, and all the locks at the company were the same, un-

less Bill had replaced his with one that was not "bumpable," although the statistic Seth had read on the Internet was, due to the high cost of good locks, most locks could be bumped. It was a reality of economics that most people could spend $30 more on a good lock to protect themselves and their valuables, but chose not to do it. . Perhaps, the common man had not done the same economic analysis as industry does with their products. For example, when a product showed a particular dangerous defect, such as an exploding gas tank, industry would run actuary tables on the estimated amount it would cost to make the product safe, versus the amount they would have to pay out in product liability defense and settlements, and opt for the cheapest alternative. Maybe it was cheaper to save money on the locks in the short run, or maybe insurance companies should give premium rebates to make up the difference in the higher cost lock. Seth found himself occupied with these mental tangents in between break-in attempts.

Seth vowed to himself that this would be the night, and he still had enough time to get into Bill's office and do what needed to be done without arousing suspicion. A trip to the restroom normally followed not too long after a coffee trip so he figured he would keep repeating the process until he got in.

Seth waited what he thought was the appropriate amount of time for his return pass at Bill's office. Seeing nobody in the corridor, he put the bump key in, gave it a smack, and nothing. Again, he heard footsteps approaching so he decided to give it a harder whack, and, if that did not work, he would abort the mission until the next opportunity. The echo of footsteps was getting louder and louder. This time he decided not to be shy and kept tapping and trying to move the bump key until, finally, it turned, and Seth slipped in.

It was either civil disobedience or his first act of criminality. The law was relative. The genocide by man of thousands of species, even one gene off from his own, was never considered a crime, and the criminals went unpunished. Whoever blew the whistle on this latest assault to the environment was more likely to be a criminal than a hero. Mother Nature was a great equalizer. No matter how powerful man dreamed to become, she could equalize it all with a few strategically placed earthquakes, floods, or both. It seemed that she was patient. She would let man kill themselves off. The earth would be reborn again, and a new species would eventually become the new rapers and pillagers of the planet.

CHAPTER 29

Once inside Bill's office, Seth breathed a sigh of relief. As he locked the door behind him, he became aware for the first time that he was sweating profusely, not only from his brow, but also from the palms of his hands as well. He definitely was a better scientist than a criminal and made a mental note to thank his parents for helping him with his higher education and to especially thank his father for suggesting it.

Seth powered up Bill's computer, and, as he was waiting for it to boot up, went through his desk drawers, which were all unlocked and revealed nothing, except for one. The desk lock was even simpler to bump than the door, and Seth was prepared with a bump key for that as well, modeled after the key to his own desk drawer. He kept the lights off in Bill's office to avoid arousing suspicion and used a small flashlight to see.

Seth looked through each file in the "secret drawer." Interestingly, there was a government issued directory of every employee at the EPA. There was a file with handwritten notes of conversations with EPA administrators. Seth photographed the notes with his cell phone. Then Seth came across an unexpected find - a file folder with internal EPA reports and one with internal FDA reports.

There was a report from the FDA on the dangers of the use of the CaMV virus as a promoter in genetic engineering, outlining the danger of horizontal transfer of the promoter to reactivate dormant viruses, and the potential to create even new viruses. The CaMV virus was the company's choice, not because it was the only choice to activate the foreign GMO gene implants to produce the desired traits, but it was the easiest. The report warned of possible abnormal cell formation in the stomach and colon, a precursor to cancer. Seth photographed the report.

Seth did not expect to find such a treasure trove of information. He was mainly there to see if his own report had been communicated to anyone in the government, and he had not even looked in Bill's computer files yet. They would be a lot easier to copy than shooting photographs, page by page, of the hard copy of a lengthy government report.

There was a report from Bill while he was Deputy Commissioner of the FDA about why milk from cows who had been given the genetically engineered growth hormone, rBGH, did not need to be labeled. To make rBGH, the company inserted a cow's growth hormone gene into E. Coli bacteria. It was then injected into dairy cows' bloodstreams to increase their production of milk. Of course, this report was common knowledge so Seth didn't have to copy it. The CaMV report had, apparently, not seen its way past Bill's desk drawer.

There were records of Bill's meetings with the U.S. Vice President. Seth didn't have time to study them, opting to photograph them and read them later. They had to do with "reducing regulatory burden." With regard to genetically engineered foods, the company practically regulated itself. It submitted reports to the FDA which were regularly and habitually rubber stamped by the regulators. It was difficult to determine which side of the revolving door the FDA regulators were on and which side the company's officials were on, and some of them moved between the two camps as often as someone would move up the ranks in promotion. The same was true with the EPA, the other regulator of company products.

The lax on regulation was touted as "reforms" to get better agricultural products to farmers and consumers but, again, this was common knowledge for anyone who cared to look into it. While Bill had been Deputy Commissioner of the FDA, he had been responsible for formulating some of the current policies concerning genetically engineered foods still in use today - that GM foods are no riskier than any others, and that the FDA had no information to the contrary, and if a GMO food were the nutritional equivalent of its ordinary counterpart, it was generally recognized as safe (or GRAS). Seth wondered what Bill would say if he were back at the FDA now that he had reviewed Seth's report on Bt corn.

As he dug deeper, the smell of corruption became even stronger. Contrary to the general statement of safety, the FDA's own microbiologist had submitted reports that genetic engineering was profoundly different than traditional breeding and summarized the dangerous effects of GM foods that may not become apparent until many years later.

There was a toxicology report warning of high concentrations of plant toxins which justified a full toxicology study, which, of course, never occurred. There was a report recommending the testing of each GM food before it is exposed to the public, pointing out that residues of plant constituents or toxins in meat and milk products may pose human food safety concerns.

There was a memo from FDA scientists on the use of the antibiotic resistant marker gene, warning of the dangers of introducing the gene into the flora of the general population in creating possible resistances to common antibiotics.

Finally, the biggest prize of all - a report on the toxicity of the Bt toxin as produced by genetically engineered plants, and it was not Seth's report. It was an EPA report that explained why nerdy little Richard Roberts had been sneaking around lately. He must have been reporting to Bill. Seth photographed the report and casually glanced at his watch to check the time. He had already been in Bill's office for an hour and had not even read one file from his computer. Seth had to work fast, or he would surely be caught.

CHAPTER 30

Seth quickly powered up Bill's computer and temporarily reset his password so he could use it. The first thing he did was load a spyware program into the computer that allowed him to access the computer remotely from his office and monitor everything that Bill did while he was logged in, including his emails. Next, he began the tedious task of looking through every file folder for anything damaging, especially for electronic copies of the paper reports he had just seen. Seth copied whatever looked suspicious onto his flash drive.

Time seemed to be running faster now than it did before, and Seth was so anxious that he found himself worrying more about getting caught than getting what he had worked so hard to get. Then, suddenly, he heard a key turning in the lock on Bill's door. Seth quickly switched the monitor off but didn't have time to kill the computer, which kept quietly humming, and he dove under Bill's desk just as the janitor walked into the office. Seth was wrong. They had not completed their rounds. They were late tonight. He tried to breathe more quietly; his anxiety fought the effort.

Luckily, it was Steve, the company's worst janitor. If you were unlucky enough to have Steve clean up your office, you would have dirty floors, dusty tables, and a generally messy outcome. About all Steve was capable of doing, was emptying the wastebasket. Thank God.

Steve was wearing headphones and an iPod. Seth could have had a coughing fit, and Steve never would have heard him. He breathed a sigh of relief as he watched Steve haphazardly run the vacuum randomly across the floor in no particular pattern while he danced around to the music. Seth became as still and quiet as a rock when Steve reached over behind the desk to grab the wastebasket. What would Seth say to Steve if he found him sitting there under Bill's desk? There was nothing really he could say. "Hi Steve, just sittin' here under Bill's desk in his locked office." Or how about, Steve, you do such a shitty job with cleaning that I thought I would hide and actually watch you and, if you don't start doing a better job, I'm going to report you. That was the variant that Seth would say if Steve saw him crouching there. Then he could indignantly storm out of Bill's office.

Steve set the wastebasket back, and it hit Seth's left elbow as he did. Seth was crouched under Bill's desk for what seemed an eternity. As a kid, he would have thought that this was somehow cozy. He used to make "forts" out of different materials and sit in them, in exactly the same manner he was crouched under Bill's desk. All he felt now was nervous, cramped, and uncomfortable. Finally, Steve rolled his janitor cart out of Bill's office, switched off the lights, and closed the door behind him.

Seth quickly got back to work, turning the monitor back on and looking for more buried treasure. Not only did he find the electronic copies of the FDA and EPA reports, he also found his own, fully-equipped with comments that Bill had made on the document itself. It was enough information to indict Bill and the company for serious criminal activity and enough to kill any aspirations Bill may have had of being in politics. He had been through the revolving door so many times Seth supposed that Bill took his close relationship with the government for granted, and that was his mistake.

Seth temporarily suppressed his knee-jerk reaction to close the computer and go now that he had found what he was looking for, but he decided, "What the hell, I've come this far, might as well do a thorough job." After another half hour of digging through files, the effort paid off. Seth uncovered a document marked "Classified." It appeared to be a report covering results on other genetic insertions of not only insecticide type agents, but agents developed from viruses, bacteria, and fungus that could be inserted into plants to cross pollinate with and eradicate coca and opium poppy plants in regions like Afghanistan, Cambodia, Laos, Thailand, Colombia, Bolivia and Peru. The report's premise was that this technology could be helpful for the development of biological weapons, and that is why it was marked as classified.

The report came as a shock to Seth. Once a deadly virus or toxin was inserted into the particular ecosystem where the drug producing plants were to be eradicated, the plants could contaminate other plants or animals, or even the entire ecosystem. Many of these drug-producing areas, such as Colombia, were adjacent to or even hidden among rainforests. Rainforests cover only a small part of the earth but produce most of the world's oxygen. The rainforest, which included Colombia, is called the "Lungs of the Earth," because it produces approximately 20% of the world's oxygen. To allow the intrusion of a drug fighting GMO into this ecosystem could be devastating to the world's environment. To allow the technology to be used for biological warfare would be disastrous to say the least.

Seth took another "once over" of all the folders in Bill's computer, making a note to double check and make sure that he had not missed anything when he remotely accessed the computer from his office. He powered off the computer and monitor, stood up, and was about to leave when the door opened again, and once more he dove under the desk. It was Steve again, out to cure his reputa-

tion as the worst janitor on earth. Now he apparently had decided to pretend to dust the office furniture. Seth watched Steve's feet from under the desk as he moved around the office, perfunctorily dusting with his feather duster to the music playing between his ears. Then the feet were right in front of him as Steve dusted Bill's desk and computer. Seth could see the Nike logos on Steve's sneakers and his one floppy untied lace. They were so close to his view. So close that, if Steve had moved his feet an inch closer, he would have kicked Seth. This time under the desk seemed even longer. Then something happened that was even worse. Steve sat down in Bill's chair and popped open a Coke. He was taking a break. Seth curled up and waited for the laziest janitor in the world to finish his coffee break.

CHAPTER 31

When Steve finally left the office, Seth had to pull his body out from under the desk one limb at a time, like a contortionist. His legs had gone to sleep, and he had to rub the painful tingles out of them to make them function again. He carefully opened the door a pinch and looked both ways down the corridor before he slipped out and went in the direction of the restroom.

That night, while lying in bed looking at the ceiling, expecting another bout of insomnia, something wonderful happened. Seth realized that, when he began to have incredibly ridiculous and illogical thoughts, his brain was finally putting him to sleep. Insomnia? Forget about Ambien, try burglary.

Seth woke with the power of clear thought for the first time in weeks. Now that he had all this evidence, he had to analyze it and, more importantly, he had to decide what to do with it. He felt like Daniel Ellsberg must have felt when he had the Pentagon papers in his hands, but Seth worked for Germinat. His move would either be interpreted as whistle-blowing, for which he would receive praise and possibly a reward, or, since the government and the powerful people who ran it were implicated, he could be regarded as a "traitor." Seth hoped that the general public would come to his support, but that hope was naïve since most people didn't know what genetically engineered foods were, let alone the fact that they were all eating them.

Seth needed an escape plan in case he became a criminal instead of a hero. Someplace where the overreaching arms of the United States government could not get to him. Brazil? Nope. Brazil had an extradition treaty with the United States, and, according to the Internet, so did every major country so, unless

*he wanted to go to a nice warm place like Afghanistan or Iran,
he had some thinking to do. He needed to pick a place far away
but one that he could reach on a non-stop flight from the United
States. The U.S. checks you into the country, but they don't yet
track your movements out of it. He would be able to get out of the
country, but he didn't want to be stuck in a foreign country that
allowed extradition if he became a hot potato.*

 *It had to be a country where the people looked somewhat simi-
lar to Americans so he could blend in, and that ruled out all of the
African and Middle Eastern countries. Strangely enough, Russia
had a good ring to it. It was far away and an old enemy of the
United States. The population was somewhat eclectic, but there
were a lot of Caucasians like Seth living there, and he may be able
to blend in; however, there was the language barrier. Seth spoke
no Russian at all. His chances for political asylum there seemed to
be pretty good. There was a non-stop to Moscow on Aeroflot Russian airlines from Washington, DC. He just had to get to DC, and
then he was home free. Russia seemed to be the best choice.*

 *When Seth headed for the office the next day, he was as para-
noid as a coke addict. On the drive to work, he constantly checked
the mirrors to see if someone were following him. When he got to
work, he nervously panned the scene from side to side and looked
over his shoulder. As he entered the lab, Dan Harkavy sensed his
unease and asked, "Seth, are you alright?"*

 "Fine Dan, just fine. Why would I not be all right?"

 "You just look a little preoccupied, that's all."

 *Seth had to get himself together if he were going to pull this
off. People might suspect he was on drugs or even worse. He had to
play it cool. Dan was continuing to work with Seth on the Mira-*

cle Rice program which was good because a human robot like Dan was all the company Seth could stand right now.

"Seth, I still don't know what makes this stuff better than carrots," said Dan. "They can't grow carrots in Africa and India?"

Dan had a point. This stuff produced hardly any beta-carotene, and it was yet to be seen if cooking would even destroy the little it did produce. How could the shit be better than growing carrots? Seth already had taken on more than he could chew.

"The theory is that rice is the only thing they eat so carrots, although a great idea, is not thought to be a solution. We just have to get the levels of beta carotene up and make sure the nutrients are there and get absorbed after cooking."

Seth was sounding like a company man again, but he knew, in just a short while, all of that would be over. No more yacht parties in St. Tropez. No more company car, and getting fired would be the easiest part of it all.

Seth pretended to work as he poured over the files from Bill's computer on the flash drive. His spyware program was working brilliantly, and he was able to pick up every key stroke that Bill made on his computer, including his emails. Would Bill be so stupid, or so bold, as to email the EPA directly, even though email could be easily hacked? Seth did find a dialogue with Roberts going back at least two months. An ongoing and continuing contact about the "independent" Bt testing.

Most of the emails were pretty innocuous, but there was one from Bill to Roberts that Seth found most revealing. "Team 1's tests with live rats were run simultaneously with Team 2's test tube tests. The rat tests had positive results for toxicity but were discredited due to abnormal lab conditions and breaches in containment." Abnormal lab conditions? Breaches in containment?

"Team 2's tests were conducted with simulated digestive acids and were completely negative."

With the EPA's own scientists' report on the Bt toxin which had been scrapped by Bill and Roberts, and this email, Seth had enough evidence to take down the whole corrupt scheme. There remained only two things to be done - to figure out who to talk to and how to stay out of jail long enough to have the opportunity.

CHAPTER 32

Pallazo was an elegant, European style restaurant on the outskirts of town. It was there that they arranged to meet Dave Salisbury (or whatever his name was) and his wife Julia. Seth and Natasha arrived together with Yuri and his date Lena. Yuri's choice was just as Seth had expected - a tall blonde model type with smoky, turquoise eyes. The four of them had a seat in Pallazo's dimly lighted dining room where they were offered an aperitif. Seth and the girls sipped on a glass of champagne as Yuri matched, what seemed like each sip of champagne they took, with a full shot of vodka while they waited for their guests to arrive.

After about fifteen minutes, in walked Dave and Julia. Dave Salisbury, on the surface, looked like a guy who could never be married. He was a playboy type in his late 30s and a sharp dresser, tonight being no exception. Dave wore a designer sports jacket and chic designer jeans; not at all what you would expect from an FBI agent's undercover expense budget. His wife (or whoever she was), Julia, was a conservative dresser with more of what you would expect an FBI agent to be wearing. She had mousy, brown hair, spoke in nasal tones, and was somewhat frumpy - not much to look at. They went together about as well as Brad Pitt and a den mother from Davenport, Iowa.

Once seated, the girls began chatting among themselves, and the gentlemen began their mutual inquisitions.

" Are you a Canucks fan, Dave?" asked Seth.

"Uh, yeah, yeah."

" I am too. I never miss a game when I'm back home. I've got season tickets at the Rogers."

It was obvious that Dave didn't know a Canuck from a schnook. After Seth showed he knew enough about Vancouver (from studying it on the Internet) to blow Dave's cover if he gave the wrong answer to something, the talk turned, oddly enough, to something that Seth really did know.

"Do we have to worry in this restaurant about being served genetically modified food?" asked Dave.

"They don't have that shit in Russia," said Yuri.

"Well, they have it in Canada, and I, for one, am no fan of it. How about you George?"

"Never really gave it a second thought," said Seth.

"You don't care if you could be eating poisonous food?"

"You only live once," said Seth.

"Does it ever bother you – you know, the close-knit relationship between the U.S. government and the biotech companies?" asked Dave.

"Why should it?" said Seth. "I'm Canadian."

" The biotech companies are U.S. based, and it seems like they practically run the FDA, doesn't it?"

Seth was getting very uncomfortable but tried to keep eye contact with Dave to avoid letting on that he was nervous. Yuri changed the subject.

"Guys, this is boring. Why don't we order dinner and, maybe after dinner, we can go to nightclub? What do you think, girls? You want to go to nightclub?"

The girls were all for it The GMO discussion was tabled for its lack of excitement, and Yuri signaled for the waiter.

After dinner, the group went to Chic, the hottest nightclub in town. There the drinking continued, and Seth was beginning to get a dizzy feeling from trying to match shots with Dave and Yuri. A cardinal rule for a foreigner living in Russia is to never try to drink like a Russian man, unless, of course, you happen to be one. A Russian man will drink you under the table every time. Yuri was sitting next to Lena, and, although she was a perfectly fine specimen to stare at, Yuri's eyes followed every chick who walked into the club with the proficiency of a bird's rotating neck. That was to be expected of Yuri, but Dave was also doing the same thing while he was sitting right next to his wife. Seth was saved from further inquisition by Dave because the music was so loud you would have to be a lip reader to have a conversation.

The girls were oblivious to the gentlemen's sport of girl watching as they continued to babble with one another about shoes, purses, and makeup, and then they got up together and disappeared into the smoke and lights onto the crowded dance floor together for a "girl dance." With their newfound freedom, Yuri and Dave also mingled onto the floor. Soon Natasha returned alone.

"Where are the girls?" asked Seth.

"Lena went to the bathroom, and Julia just disappeared."

Natasha sat down and had to speak right into Seth's ear to be heard over the music, giving him another taste of that pleasant "ear tickle." Seth reached for his glass and, as he did, he saw a mousy-haired girl rubbing up against a young guy on the dance floor.

"Isn't that her there?" he said to Natasha.

"No, it couldn't be."

"Yeah, yeah, that's her. I'll be damned!"

If Julia had not had all her clothes on, it would have been a strip tease. She was writhing, pulling up her shirt, and wrapping herself around the guy's body like he was her dance pole.

"I wonder what Dave would think if he saw that?" asked Seth.

"I think he's in solidarity with her," said Natasha, pointing to a far corner of the room where dapper Dave was pushing up against a beautiful, Russian blonde girl against the wall, making out with her like a teenage kid.

Yuri returned to the table with Lena. As he did, Julia and her dance partner disappeared into the smoke, and Dave led his newfound toy off into the corridor.

"What you guys are looking at?" asked Yuri.

"Oh, nothing," said Seth.

After a while, an openly drunk Julia staggered back to the table, but she didn't even ask where Dave was. When Dave finally returned, he looked like all he needed was a cigarette to celebrate the climax of his orgasmic festivities.

"Isn't this place great?" asked Dave.

"Yeah, but it's about 4 a.m., and we should be getting back home," said Seth.

"You guys go ahead. I stay," said Yuri. So much for Seth's protection from the FBI.

As the four of them were exiting the club, two young drunk idiots came out of the shadows, one of them screaming in Russian what was very clear to Seth to be a stream of obscenities.

"What are they saying?" Seth asked Natasha.

"He says to Dave to stay away from his girlfriend if he wants to live."

Now it was clear that Dave was the cause of the problem, and he was not showing any sign of backing down to them. In fact, he went right up to them and got in their faces, surprisingly, yelling his own stream of Russian expletives.

"Dave tells the punks to go away, or they will be sorry."

In the next split second, one of the punks grabbed Dave, slipping his arm underneath Dave's in a half-Nelson hold while the other punk pulled out a knife and made slashing movements with it, advancing toward Dave. No sooner could Seth even think of coming to his aid, Dave clamped down on the holding punk's arm, pushed away from him, lifted his waist in the air, and kicked the oncoming attacker in the chest, sending the holder flying and the attacker falling, and the knife clattered to the ground. Dave then stood up in a martial arts ready stance and faced both of his opponents who scrambled to reset their balance and run away. Then Dave picked up the knife, pocketed it and turned around. Just like James Bond, he smiled and brushed off his expensive designer jacket.

"Now that the excitement's over, can I walk you guys home?"

Seth didn't know whether to feel safe or terrified by that offer.

CHAPTER 33

Dave and Julia were either swingers, or they were not married at all, and Dave was obviously trained in martial arts and had no fear.

"Did you check him out?" Seth asked Yuri.

"He is FBI agent assigned to public corruption division."

That sounded like a far cry from tracking down fugitives, but it could have been just a layer of cover so nobody from the outside could find out his real assignment.

"What are we going to do?"

"Nothing."

"Nothing?"

"Look, we don't know for sure if this guy is after you or even suspects who you are. We observe him for now. I don't think he poses any danger for you."

"You're the expert."

Seth played along with Yuri, but he didn't think that waiting and observing was good enough. He had to be proactive. To be on guard, it was better to know what you were guarding against. That meant more spying, and it was going to be a lot more difficult to spy on a trained FBI agent than it was to spy on Bill Penner. He was going to need a bigger bag of tricks.

Seth began pondering his moves in his daily thoughts. He had to figure out a way to get invited to Dave's apartment. That way, he could see what kind of a lock he had in order to figure out how to pick it. Getting into his apartment and searching it and his computer was the only way to find out what Dave was really doing.

At work, Seth gave 1,000 rubles to the records administrator to obtain access to Dave's file. In the file was a copy of his false passport, a copy of his degrees and academic record (also false), and a host of bogus testimonials about his teaching abilities, but Seth was more interested in the inside cover. It contained his address and telephone number, as well as some medical information. Seth jotted down the address and phone numbers, as well as emergency contact information.

Seth located Dave's apartment on the map and took off from work early to scope out the neighborhood. It was not very far from his own. There was a small coffee shop right across the street from his building that would make a good vantage point for the surveillance. Seth took a seat in the coffee shop, ordered a cup of coffee, and contemplated his next move.

Every Russian apartment had several main entrance doors or podyezd, each had a staircase to service several apartments on each floor. Seth left the coffee shop, walking by the building to identify which door belonged to Apartment 2 which was Dave's apartment.

Getting past the security of the building would be easy. It was a simple intercom buzzer with which any occupant of an apartment could "buzz-in" visitors and open the door. He would just randomly ring several of Dave's neighbors to tell them he was from the water company and needed to get into the building. Somebody who was too lazy to check or too irritated to stand another ring of the doorbell would buzz him in. Next, he would have to pick the lock on the door of the apartment, and then he would be inside. It would have to happen at a time when Dave was at work. Seth would call in sick, break into the apartment, and there would be no chance of getting caught by Dave.

The only variable was Julia. For that, he needed to study the patterns of her daily comings and goings. Seth would have to call in sick for about a week so he could spend at least a few days of surveillance before the break-in. It would be nice to get a good look at the door to the apartment so he could determine how to pick the lock. There were some kids playing in the play yard, so he walked over to the play yard and hung around until he saw them moving toward the door to go inside.

Seth slipped in behind the children who disappeared up the stairs into another apartment. He cautiously walked up the stairs to the second apartment, which was one of four that faced the staircase. If Julia should open the door, he could turn around and run down the one short flight of stairs and out the door without being recognized. His fur hat and bulky coat would disguise him enough to look like any other Russian man. Of course, that theory didn't work if he were nose-to-nose with her door lock at the time. The door, at first glance, looked like a cheap, Chinese-made door that could be easily picked. He approached the door closer, and, with each step, he could feel his heart beating faster and faster.

Seth's examination of the door was not as fruitful as his initial observation. The door was a Chinese door, but it had been outfitted with a formidable looking lock. The lock appeared to fit a very thick key. It was definitely not bumpable. This would be tough to crack. Seth wrote down the brand of the lock - ABLOY PROTEC. He would have to look up the lock on the Internet to see the prescribed way to open it without the key.

Seth escaped from the apartment, only to see Julia walking toward him about 100 meters away with two bags of groceries. He quickly turned his back to her and walked away, hoping that he had not been seen as he headed off in the other direction.

CHAPTER 34

The Abloy Protec lock was a high-security lock, with over 1 billion possible combinations and, as luck would have it, was pick proof and bump proof. The manufacturer advertised them as superior, mechanical locks, suitable for hospitals, universities and large industrial and government complexes. A lock hack site recommended "impressioning" as the only way to open them.

Impressioning was a method of taking a mold of a key in clay or silicone and then pouring epoxy, silicone, or low-melting point metal into the mold, thus making a new key. For that, he would have to figure out a way to obtain Dave's key long enough to make the mold. In anticipation, Seth bought some clay and a box he could put the clay in to make the mold. The next step was getting the keys away from Dave to make the impression and putting them back before he noticed.

Dave was a trained FBI agent, and Seth didn't think he was going to be easily tricked into giving up his keys. There had to be a way to do it without arousing suspicion.

Day after day, Seth observed Dave and his habits and, in his free time, he staked out Dave and Julia's apartment to observe Julia's comings and goings. Calling in sick to perform intense surveillance was useless until he had the key for the impression. He kept his impression box in his jacket pocket at all times in case he would have the opportunity. Unfortunately, that opportunity never came.

Time was moving forward, and Seth had not made any progress toward his goal of finding out why Dave was there and what it had to do with him. Finally, he decided that the best way was to get Dave back to the club where he seemed to be in his element and slip some GHB - gamma-hydroxybutyric acid in his drink. GHB was often referred to as the "date rape drug." Once given to a subject, it knocked them out almost immediately and was virtually undetectable 8 to 12 hours later. Seth would challenge Dave to a "drinking contest." Then, when Dave was not looking, he would slip the GHB into his drink. When Dave passed out, Seth would call for an ambulance and, while Dave was at the hospital being pronounced drunk, Seth would make the impression of his key.

Seth had to bribe a local pharmacist with 10,000 rubles to obtain the GHB. Now he could proceed with his plan to make the duplicate key.

Seth knew that Dave, unlike most of his colleagues who used public transportation, had a car so he hung out in the parking lot every day after work. One day, as luck would have it, Seth ran into Dave after class when he was getting into his car. Most foreigners didn't have cars in Khabarovsk, but Dave had a very nice Lexus SUV which must have set the government back a few bucks because premium cars in Russia cost about double what they did in Europe.

"Hey, Dave."

"Oh. Hey, George. Can I give you a ride?"

"Sure, great."

Seth hopped into the SUV and was immediately greeted by that "new car smell." He wondered why the bureau had allowed Dave to pick such an expensive car for himself. It had four-wheel drive and all the luxuries, like a kick-ass sound system, beautiful leather seats and trim, radar equipped bumpers, and a rearview camera. If he didn't know any better, Seth would think that this was one of the cars of the Germinat group.

"Dave, I was wondering if you wanted to do another club night? This time, um, without the girls."

"George, I didn't know you had it in you."

"It's okay, I mean, with your wife?"

"What? Oh, yeah, fine, okay. When were you thinking of?"

"Friday night?"

Dave dropped Seth off at his apartment building. He had no intention of telling Yuri of his covert operation because he would never tolerate it. Seth was on his own. He had a copy of the spyware he had used on Bill's computer. He planned to get into the apartment, open up Dave's computer, get whatever he could in a period of half an hour, and then load the spyware for later remote access. He would have to work quickly because he had no idea when Julia would come home.

CHAPTER 35

Friday night is a universally wild night. All the tensions of the work week are bottled up all week long and tightly corked. The pressure builds each day until, toward Friday afternoon, everyone feels lazy and impatiently keeps their eyes on the clock. Finally, there is an explosion of freedom, but, for Seth, it was just another work day - teacher work, then spy work. Spy work was more exciting but also the most nerve wracking, and the pay was not too alluring either.

At about midnight, the Chic nightclub started to come alive. Beautiful, scantily-clad women who had worked for hours fixing their hair, makeup, and selecting just the right outfit would soon engage in a massive competition. Their prize was a snappily dressed and well-groomed young man who was in the process of transforming himself into a horny drunk by the night's end. Into this overplayed scene walked Dave and Seth. Dave, of course, was expertly dressed and ready for an evening of prowling.

Dave had popped the cork on Friday and was ready for an early start. He ordered a bottle of vodka for the table and invited every girl who walked by to sit down. Some did, politely for a few minutes, but it would take just a little more alcohol consumption to complete Seth's plan.

Dave spilled the vodka bottle over two shot glasses, filling them to the brim with the dexterity of a skilled bartender. Lifting his glass, he said, "Nosdaroviya, George."

They clicked glasses and began to imitate the Russian male game of slamming vodka, which was kind of like chain smoking with the violent death assured to come much sooner.

"I'm glad we could get away tonight," said Seth.

" I am too. George, why don't you grab yourself a girl?"

Dave motioned with his nose at a tall strawberry blonde in a sequined mini skirt.

"Grab one?"

"Yeah, grab her."

"I can't grab her."

"Okay, then I will."

Dave promptly got up, went over to the girl, and, smiling, took her by the arm to their table.

"What's your name, honey?"

"I don't speak English. Sorry."

Whereupon Dave went into perfect Russian, weaving a thick web of charm that she had no hope from which to escape. He flagged down a waiter and ordered a bottle of champagne.

"George, this is Svetlana. Now you go get one for yourself."

"Oh no, I...."

"Who's the science teacher, you or I? I thought I was sup- posed to be the nerd."

"You're the farthest thing from a nerd, Dave."

"Okay then, I'll get you one."

The thought of that was disastrous to Seth. If there was someone at the table watching his every move, there was no way he could drop the GHB into Dave's drink.

"No, no, Dave, just take Svetlana to dance and by the time you come back, I'll have one."

This must have sounded good to Dave who took his girl onto the dance floor and disappeared into the riotous mist that was the center of the club.

Seth had to work fast. He filled each shot glass to the top, leaving enough room to slip the GHB into Dave's glass, looked around to see if anyone were watching him, and dropped the contents of the GHB vial into Dave's drink. Since Svetlana was drinking champagne, there was no danger of confusing glasses. Next Seth had to complete his promise to Dave. He looked around the room, figuring that the sluttiest looking girl would probably be the easiest one to bring to the table. The problem was there were no available sluts. All the sluts had already taken their positions at other tables - low lying fruit. Seth's task would be a real challenge. Not only did he not care about getting a female companion because he had a perfectly good one already, but this fact would show in his body language, mannerisms, and make it less likely he would be successful in picking up another one.

Seth slammed a shot of vodka for courage, refilled his glass, and stood up, walking straight to the first girl he saw who was not hanging around any friends. She was of average height, brunette, dressed well, but not too revealing, in a pretty, black cocktail dress. Taking her gently by the arm, he said, "Darling, you are, by far, the most beautiful girl in this room. I must take you back to my table for a closer look, or I will always regret it."

The girl was charmed, smiled, and gave up resistance to Seth's grip. As they approached the table, Dave was returning with Svetlana, and they were both laughing. They all sat, and Seth's girl introduced herself as Masha.

"That's my boy!" said Dave. "What are you drinking, sweetheart?" Dave asked Masha.

"Vodka." Wrong answer. She was supposed to drink champagne like Svetlana.

"Here," said Dave, shoving his fully loaded date rape shot glass toward her. "Take mine."

Just as Masha attempted to grip the glass, Seth slid it back to Dave saying "It's okay. I'll get her a clean one," when the unthinkable happened. The glass spilled all over the table.

As the evening wore on, out of necessity, Seth created a system for drinking without getting drunk. As the men slammed their vodka (Masha sipped), Seth took the entire load of vodka in his mouth, then went for a sip of grapefruit juice, spitting the vodka into the juice glass while he pretended to drink it to wash down the vodka. That way, he could stay sober, keep his wits about him, and not miss the next opportunity to slip Dave a mickey.

As the night turned into morning, Dave was doing a pretty good job at drugging himself into unconsciousness without any help. Seth began to worry about combining the GHB with so much alcohol. In the beginning, after a few drinks, it was pretty safe, but now Dave had consumed over half a liter of vodka and showed no signs of stopping anytime soon. Seth would have to abort, unless Dave got sauced to the point he couldn't see straight. Then he would simply turn over his keys to Seth voluntarily with no suspicion.

Dave wallowed in a drunken stupor for the next two hours, getting up to stumble to the bathroom from time to time. On the way back from the bathroom the last time, he practically fell onto the table and almost missed his seat. "This place sucks. Let's go somewhere more qui...quiet, more quiet." Dave's words tumbled and rolled around in his mouth and flapped through his lips in the same random drunken manner as he walked. It's amazing how ridiculous a drunk man looks and has no clue how stupid he looks to others who are sober.

"Well, what do you say guys? Let's get out of here," said Dave.

Dave slurred a few misguided phrases that Seth thought were supposed to be romantic to Svetlana in Russian. Seth was sure that she would have nothing to do with him, but, to his surprise, she accepted his invitation. Dave waved his arms in the air for the waiter like he was doing aerobics or guiding a 747 into the gate.

"Can you come with us?" Seth said to Masha. "I promise I won't try anything. I just don't want to leave my friend alone. It will be a couple of hours at the most."

Graciously, she accepted, and the four left in search of the nearest motel. They didn't wander for long. The Hollywood Palace Hotel right across the street was owned by the same proprietor as Chic. The music from Chic was so loud it could be felt in the lobby while they were checking in. They booked two rooms next to each other and ordered some fruit and more champagne. Astonishingly enough, Dave also bought another bottle of vodka.

The groans of drunk men and women faking orgasms from the other rooms permeated the paper thin walls of Dave's room where they began to socialize as a precursor to more intimate activities. His room was a deluxe "suite" with gaudy chartreuse wallpaper, a cheap velour couch, and two armchairs. The center of the room had a huge, king-size bed that could fit at least three women and one man, and probably often did.

The girls cut fruit while Dave slammed a few nightcaps. As Masha and Seth munched on slices of orange and apple, Dave, whose charm machine was definitely out of order, began pawing at Svetlana's boobs and slurring what he must have thought were Russian sweet nothings in her ear. Seth could only imagine the promises that must have been made to cap the night off with the discovery of whether Dave could actually finish this elaborate performance. As he wrapped his arm around Svetlana and leaned into her face, practically falling into her lap, he motioned with his free hand for Seth and Masha to leave, as if he were swatting at a fly.

Seth and Masha left with a bottle of champagne and some fruit and went to the room next door. Masha was pleasant and nice. She had pretty, brown eyes which could not hide her embarrassment. They made small talk as they tried not to pay attention to the headboard in Dave's room thumping against the wall and the phony screams of ecstasy of Svetlana mixed with the guttural groans of Dave until, finally, everything went silent.

After a while, they heard a knock on the door. It was Svetlana. Dave had passed out cold in the bed. Seth arranged for a taxi for both girls and promised to see Dave home safely, taking his room key from Svetlana. It was a lucky break he had not expected.

Once inside Dave's room, Seth could hear Dave snoring like a bear as he rifled through his pockets. There was his fake Canadian passport, his Russian registration which conveniently had his address on it, which would defer any suspicion as to how Dave got home that night, and, finally, his keys. The multi-faceted three dimensional Abloy key stood out from all the others. Seth took the keys into the bathroom, withdrew his clay box, lubricated Dave's key, and made an impression of both sides of it. The hard part was done.

As dawn was breaking, Seth showed up on Julia's doorstep with Dave slung over his shoulder like a golf bag. Surprisingly, Julia had absolutely no reaction to Dave's behavior, as though she either didn't care or it was normal.

"How did you find the apartment?" she asked.

"I just looked at his registration."

"George, I'm really sorry about this."

"No worries. He'll sleep it off."

CHAPTER 36

Seth was making love to Natasha in his bed and all was very pleasant until he heard a faint knocking. *Was that the front door?* He continued making love to her, but the knocking gained in intensity until it turned to pounding, and Seth opened his pasty, sleepy eyes, rubbing them and looking around the room to discover he was alone in the bed.

"I'm coming," he yelled to the pounder.

Seth stumbled into the living room and corridor of his apartment, putting on his pants while shuffling to the front door and peering into the peephole, only to be startled by the vision of a large fist continuing to pound.

"Hold on. Who is it?"

As the fist drew back and stopped pounding, he saw Yuri's distorted face in the peephole.

"Great," said Seth and opened the door.

"You look like shit," said Yuri. "Where were you all last night?"

"Out with Natasha," said Seth, figuring that this lie would be easier than modifying a version of the truth.

"That's breaking rules. Did you fuck her at least?"

"No, only in my dream, and, unfortunately, you messed up the best part of that for me."

"Where did you go? Nightclub?"

"Yes."

"Next time don't go anywhere without telling me, okay?"

Seth was purposely inhospitable to Yuri. All he wanted was to go back to bed, catch up on his sleep, and then work on making his impression key.

"Okay. What time is it?"

"Ten o'clock."

"I'm going back to bed. Could you?" Seth made a sweeping motion toward the door.

"Oh... sure, but next time you have to let me know, or there will be more restrictions."

"Yes, father."

"And next time – fuck her. If you don't fuck her, you will always just be friends."

Seth shut the door after Yuri and his simple but retarded advice. He was perfectly happy with the way things were going with Natasha and felt no need to push things artificially, nor did he have any desire to be with anyone but her. He dragged himself back to the bed, falling onto it like a piece of cut timber and was out in less than five minutes.

Later, Seth awoke to Natasha's call. "Where were you last night?" she asked.

"I went out with Dave - he was trying to 'bond' with me."

"Boy's night out, huh?"

"Yeah. Why don't you come over later? We can watch a movie or something."

"Actually, I've been invited to my Aunt's house tonight for dinner. Tomorrow?"

Seth was saved. He could spend the whole day scheming.

Once Seth got going, he put the clay mold together, prepared the metallic casting material, and, when it was ready, poured it into the mold. When the casting material had set, he pulled apart the clay mold and had a perfectly molded copy of the Abloy key. He filed the rough spots softly with a round file. Now the only question was when he could use it.

CHAPTER 37

Day after day spent watching Dave's apartment from the coffee shop was tedious. This spy work definitely had no glamor in it. Seth kept a log of all of Julia's comings and goings.

One thing that he noticed from all of this surveillance was that, even though she was an average looking girl, Julia was obsessed about her hair and makeup. The multi-billion dollar cosmetics industry suddenly made sense to him. Narcissus should have been a girl.

Julia did not have a set time for her beautification activities, but she was religious about getting manicures and pedicures, having her hair done at least once a week, and, of course, shopping.

It was a puzzle for men how women never got tired of shopping, even if there was nothing to buy. In Khabarovsk, the quality of shopping was limited, yet Julia engaged in it regularly as if it were part of her work instead of a pastime. If he had doubts before about whether or not she and Dave were married, the time she spent on shopping dispelled them all. The problem with her shopping habits was that they were less predictable than her trips to the beauty salon. The time she spent in the malls was erratic – one hour here, sometimes two hours there. Sometimes she went to the malls every day, and sometimes she spent days without visiting them at all. One thing was for certain – his window of opportunity to get into Dave's apartment would have to come during one of Julia's shopping sprees.

CHAPTER 38

Seth finished up looking through all Bill's files and emails. He had discovered official internal memos from the FDA during the early 90s that had been hidden from the public, warning of the dangers of genetically modified foods during the time the FDA was formulating their policy of, "if it looks like a duck, and quacks like a duck, it must be a duck, even though it may be a duck with the genes of a turtle." How would they account for the fact that humans differ genetically from chimpanzees by only a little over 1%?

Seth poured over the warnings of the FDA's own scientists in over a dozen memos. There was Dr. Edward J. Matthews' memo warning of the dangers of production of high levels of toxicants by genetically modified plants, requiring further testing, Dr. Shibko's recommendation of toxicological studies and in vitro digestion studies, both of which were never performed, the Division of Food Chemistry's memo concerning safety issues of marker genes, and Dr. Guest's memo to Dr. James Maryanski, raising toxicological and environmental concerns - the need to demonstrate that the genetically engineered foods were safe to humans, the effect of one genetically engineered organism in a mono-diet as animal feed and its effect on animal health, the need to evaluate the toxicology of genetically engineered plant by-products, and the need to evaluate the use of antibiotic-resistant marker genes. None of these tests were ever performed. In fact, no testing was ever performed by the FDA on GMOs.

There were memos from Dr. Maryanski on labeling GMOs (which is not required) and from Dr. Maryanski and Dr. Sheldon on the potential dangers of the use of antibiotic resistant marker genes, memos on the presence of stomach lesions on rats tested for tolerance to genetically engineered tomatoes, and comments from the USDA recommending generations of safety testing, as well as memos from the Dept. of Human Health and Safety recommending the same.

Finally, Dr. Pribyl's memo summed up the essence of FDA policy that there were no differences between traditional breeding and transgenic manipulation, no unintended effects without scientific testing, and no danger of transference of genes into unintended species - all of which should have been required. Dr. Pribyl criticized that policy, stating that it read like a biotech "Redbook" instead of a scientific document.

All of these concerns were secretly pushed under the rug by the FDA when it formulated its policy under the direction of Bill Penner, of course, that GMO foods were generally recognized as safe and did not need any safety testing. The proponent of each GMO food merely had to submit reports to the FDA stating that their food was generally recognized as safe. Now Bill was trying to do the same with foods engineered with Bt toxins, even though internal reports of the EPA had concluded that the Bt foods were dangerous.

Not only were these concerns swept under the rug, but the President's Office specifically instructed the FDA to state that "The method by which food is produced or developed may, in some cases, help to understand the safety or characteristics of finished food. However, the key factors in reviewing safety concerns should be the characteristics of the food product, not the fact that new methods are used." It also stated that, "The policy statement needs to stress the role of decentralized safety reviews by producers with informal FDA consultation, only if significant safety or nutritional concerns arise." In other words, official FDA policy was being written for the biotech companies to alert the FDA as to whether a GMO food were safe. If the biotech companies said it was safe, then not even any consultation with the FDA was required.

If Seth was caught with any of these memos, he might be able to talk himself out of it. After all, they were supposedly available in response to a request for documents under the Freedom of Information Act. However, if he were caught with the memo to Bill that was marked "Classified," he could be sought for treason under the Espionage Act. Seth had to be careful to whom he disclosed the information, and he had to have his escape route planned in advance. Staying in the United States was out of the question. It was too dangerous.

Seth deleted the spyware from his computer and transferred all the new information to the flash drive and made a duplicate to hide in his jacket. If he were going to try to go to Russia, he would need a visa at the minimum. It was time to meet with someone at the Russian consulate. There was a Russian consulate in Houston, as well as the main embassy in Washington, DC. Seth decided to go for DC, but he did not dare call them from his office. After work, he purchased a telephone encryption device. He would make the call from home. It was ironic to turn to the old enemy of the U.S. for help, but it seemed like the only good option available.

CHAPTER 39

Before Seth took his one week of vacation time to visit the nation's capital, he decided to go back to the office and make sure his computer was completely clean. He also had to break back into Bill's office and remove the spyware program. The next day at work, Seth found some remnants of Bill's emails he had copied on his computer. He transferred them to the flash drive and then erased them from his hard drive. He also erased his Internet browsing history.

He replaced the hard drive with a duplicate hard drive he had created for a backup and slipped the original hard drive into his case so no data erased from the original hard drive could be recovered.

Just as he was on the final key strokes, Dan said, "Seth, did you hear?" Someone hacked into Bill's desk top, and there's a big investigation."

"Shit," thought Seth, "great timing." His plans to go to Washington had to be temporarily delayed to deal with this crisis.

Two gentlemen who looked like FBI agents were assigned to check all the computers in the building under the guise of being computer consultants. Seth was in the clear so, when the two arrived at his office and asked if they could perform "routine maintenance" on his and Daniel's desktops, they both complied. Not only did the two men have Germinat visitors' badges, they also showed orders signed by the company to perform the routine maintenance.

"Be my guest," said Seth, standing back from his computer, and one of the suits took a seat at his desk.

"This won't take long," said the suit.

As Seth went down the corridor to get a cup of coffee, he had an uneasy feeling that he had forgotten something. What was it? He poured himself a cup of coffee and sat down in the break room. Then he realized what he had forgotten - the flash drive! Suddenly, that uneasy feeling graduated to anxiety, and Seth could hardly hold his coffee cup as he made his way back to the office.

The suits were still going over his computer when he got back to the office. They had already finished with Daniel's which, of course, could not have had anything on it. Seth wondered if he had inadvertently left anything damaging on the duplicate hard drive, but, most of all, he wondered if they had found the flash drive he had stupidly left plugged into the computer. The next few minutes that passed were more like hours as Seth worried. He felt his heart beating faster and his palms sweating.

"Sir, is this your computer?" asked the suit.

"Yes," said Seth.

"Could you please tell me your password for the hard drive?"

Seth had locked his hard drive with a special password. He gave it, and the suit started to pour over Seth's hard drive for what seemed like hours. Finally, when it was over, the suit gave a suspicious look toward Seth and left the room. Seth scrambled to his seat and felt the CPU for his flash drive. It was still plugged into the USB portal. He had dodged a bullet one more time.

CHAPTER 40

Seth's plan to seek refuge in Russia was not perfect. He could not disclose the particulars of the classified report because of its potential for use in biological warfare. Clearly, he could not allow that report to fall into the wrong hands. There had to be a way to conceal it so nobody would know the details until he figured out what to do with it. However, that was something that he had to put on the back burner. Now that Bill had discovered the bug on his computer, the heat was getting too close for comfort. Seth had to make his escape route the number one priority.

Seth took a week of vacation time and flew to DC. He made sure he hit the regular tourist spots and visited all the monuments and museums he could before his appointment with representatives at the Russian Embassy. He revealed just enough information to make himself valuable to them. They provided him with a one-year visa and suggested he apply for political asylum, which he did. The visa would get him into the country for at least one year while he worked on his asylum application and tried to figure out the best and most public way to disclose the information he was holding.

Germinat's value to the government apparently went far beyond their mutual management via the revolving door, into the development of biological and, no doubt, chemical weapons as well. The release of this information would have dire consequences, not only for Germinat, but also for the U.S. government. On the plane on the way home from Washington, Seth pondered the problem of how to conceal the classified report and what was its highest and best use, which he finally decided was the equiva-

lent of an insurance policy on his life. The flight attendant walked down the aisle and stopped at his seat.

"Sir, there's an empty seat available near your friends," said the flight attendant."

"My friends?"

"Yes, they were asking the gate agent about getting a seat near you, but it seems a confirmed passenger did not make the flight, and there is one open. You can take it if you like."

"Where is it?"

"17D. It's an aisle seat, only one row in back of your friends."

"Thank you. Uh, what seats are they in?"

"They're in 16E and F."

Seth looked through the rows, but he could not see who was sitting in 16E and F. Obviously someone was following him. He had to assume that they had seen him going either into or out of the Russian Embassy. If they were from the company, he still had time to make his escape because it was Friday, and they would most likely make their report on Monday. If they were from the government, his escape route may not be so easy.

Seth must be suspected of the break-in. If that were the case, it would not be long before Bill told his buddies in the government that one of his employees had his hands on classified files that could cause an international debacle. The U.S. was already famous for dropping tons of bombs on any country that it thought was using "weapons of mass destruction." To be implicated in the development of genetically engineered biological weapons, could not be very diplomatically pleasant for the country or the current administration which was already acquiring a reputation of "Ready, aim, fire..." Seth had to find out who was following him.

He could either approach those two clowns while they were boxed into their airplane seats or wait until later when they were free to do whatever they wanted with him. He decided not to wait, mustered up his courage, and went up the aisle. He sat in the unoccupied 17D, and confronted them.

"Excuse me, gentlemen. Yes, you two, can you tell me who you work for?"

Both were dressed as tourists and did not look like FBI agents.

"Well, I don't see as that's any of your business," said the tourist in 16E.

"On the contrary, since you both are following me, it is very much my business. Now give it up, or I'll tell the captain about the terrorist threat I heard you make when you boarded the plane, and the local police in St. Louis can sort it out."

"We work for Germinat," said 16F, at the same time his partner said, "Shut up."

"Look, we don't want any trouble," said 16F. "The company is doing a routine security screening to consider you for a possible promotion."

"That's right," said 16E.

"That's why you followed me while I was on my vacation?" asked Seth.

Theirs was a lame story, but Seth knew it was all he was going to get out of them. After this, he knew he could not afford to stay a minute longer in St. Louis.

Once these two made their report to Bill, the heat would be on, and he would never be allowed to leave the country. He had to make his move now. Nobody would expect Seth to turn around and go back to Washington right away, and these two clowns would most likely not make their report until Monday morning.

It was Friday, and the bank had already closed, but it was open Saturday from 9 to 12. Tomorrow would be Seth's last day in St. Louis.

CHAPTER 41

Dawn broke on what would be Seth's last day in the city of St. Louis. Seth wouldn't miss his adopted city. Sure, he had had fun in the clubs on Washington Avenue and the hip bars and restaurants on the Delmar Loop. Those were times he would never forget. He also had spent many a moment at peace, away from the bustle of the city, biking through Forest Park, but the city was never really home to him.

"Home is where you hang your hat for a while," his dad always used to say, but St. Louis felt more like just a workplace. When he was partying away from work, it was really like a coffee break. Work was always there and was always the priority. He never really did hang his hat in St. Louis. He would miss his parents and, through this entire ordeal, had not had the time to visit them in California. The thought of possibly never seeing them again was worse than anything else. Maybe it would have been easier to stop at this point. Was all he was about to give up really worth it? Would anyone really listen or care? It was too late now. He was already a suspect and was sure to be caught eventually. Staying was no longer an option.

Seth overpacked a small bag to check in all the things he would need. He stuffed so many things into the bag that he had to sit on it to zip it up, and, when he picked it up, it felt like a ton of bricks. He would pick up the go-bag at the bank, withdraw as much cash as possible, so he could pay cash for all his tickets (leaving no credit card traces), and head straight for the airport. Seth thought about putting the .357 into the bag as well, but he knew that, in Russia, his final destination, guns were illegal so he left *it behind. He didn't need to supply any more reasons to anyone to get himself arrested.*

As he exited the apartment and entered the parking lot, he looked carefully around for anything suspicious or out of place. Everything appeared to be quiet and nobody was on the street. Seth slowly walked to his car, threw the bag in the trunk, got behind the wheel, and drove away.

As he turned the corner onto Graham Street, he noticed a gray Chevrolet sedan in his rearview mirror. Having just been followed the day before, any abnormality, even a slight one, could not be overlooked. He took a sharp right turn on Clayton Avenue. The sedan was still there. He sped up and took a left on Hampton Avenue, but the sedan was still in the rearview. This was too close for coincidence.

Seth kept ahead on Hampton, approached the next signal, and, just as it was about to turn red, hung a screeching U-turn in the intersection, floored it, and headed back the opposite direction. This move failed to shake the sedan which gave chase, followed him with a U-turn through the solid red, and swerved to avoid hitting a truck.

Seth pushed the gas pedal to the floor as he looked for an escape route. He saw the sedan in the left side mirror accelerating through traffic. Spotting a grocery store, he pulled right into the store parking lot, quickly parking as close to the entrance as he could, and went inside looking over his shoulder at his pursuers. As Seth quickly lost himself in the middle aisles, he saw 16E and F exit the gray sedan and make a swift walk into the store.

As they disappeared into the produce section, Seth left through the other exit and crept in between the cars in the parking lot to the opposite side of the gray sedan. With his keys, he depressed the valve of the rear front tire until it was completely flat and then sneaked back into the store. He grabbed a pack of gum and some snacks from the racks near the cash register and then spotted 16E and F and made sure that they had spotted him as well. He checked out and slowly walked to his car and made sure that he was being followed this time.

He watched 16E and F as they discovered their tire was flat, and 16F ran frantically back into the store. Seth got in his car and made his way to the bank, parking as close to the entrance as possible. He pulled his briefcase out of the safety deposit box and withdrew the maximum cash allowed from his account, all the while looking around for any sign of his pursuers. Seeing nobody, he left the building.

As Seth approached I64, he saw the gray sedan again in his rearview mirror, closely approaching. The stop at the bank must have given them enough time to use a can of Fix-a-Flat to fill up the tire. Seth took a sharp right on Clayton and another on Oakland Avenue, screeching another right on Macklind, through a red light, and then tried to shake his tail by weaving through the residential areas in random fashion. Finally, he doubled back to Hampton and hit I64. There was still no trace of them as he merged onto I70, and Seth breathed a huge sigh of relief.

As he exited for the airport, Seth saw, from his right side mirror, the gray sedan weaving maniacally through traffic. It was too late to take evasive maneuvers. He had already made the exit. Seth punched it, but the gray sedan gained speed and rammed his rear bumper, sending his car fishtailing off the road and onto the dirt shoulder. The car spun around, making its own dust tornado, as Seth turned toward the spin and regained control of the car.

He headed straight for the airport police station, and slid into a parking space among the police cars with his pursuers hot on his tail. Before they realized it, 16E and F's car came to a screeching halt in front of the police station, and several police officers who were heading for their vehicles looked up at them. Seth waved to a policeman.

"Officer, these guys were chasing me. I passed them on I64, and they got pissed off. I think it's some kind of road rage. One of them waved a gun out the window."

That was it for 16E and F. One officer came over to him to take a report while two officers headed toward the gray sedan as it backed up in an attempt to leave. The officers signaled the sedan to stop, but it kept backing up. They drew their weapons and took a firing stance, and the car stopped.

"Out of the car. Hands on your heads!" said one officer to 16E and F.

Seth was stuck giving reports in the airport police station for the next hour. When they finally let him go, he headed for long-term parking at the United Airlines terminal.

Relieved, but still shaken, Seth got out of the car in the park-ing lot, holding his briefcase, and got the small heavy suitcase out of his trunk. He opted for the stairs because he didn't want to be trapped in any close spaces, like the elevator. It would be hard to carry the heavy case down the stairs but even worse to be cornered in an elevator. As he turned to descend the last flight of stairs, he almost ran into Bill who was below him, a pistol trained right on him.

"Seth, you are so predictable," said Bill, with one of his famous toothy grins. Seth looked around – nowhere to run – Bill was blocking the only way out.

CHAPTER 42

Sunday night could not come soon enough. Seth was ready for a break from the madness of what his life had become, and Natasha was just what he needed. She arrived around 6 pm with two bags of groceries.

"What's this?" asked Seth.

"Well, it's not really much now, but it will be our dinner."

"Dinner sounds good. What is it?"

"Russian borscht, my mom's recipe."

Natasha set the groceries down in the kitchen as Seth approached her from behind. He hugged her and pressed his face into her back. Her smell was alluring and enticing. Every moment that Seth spent with Natasha was precious to him, and she was becoming more and more important to him every day.

"Were you ever planning on introducing me to your parents?" asked Seth, turning her around and slipping his hands around her waist. He tenderly kissed her on the lips.

"Only if it gets serious," said Natasha, turning her attention away from the groceries and returning the kiss.

"It is serious," said Seth, continuing the kiss. Seth felt so close to her, it was as if they shared the same breath. Natasha finally pulled away.

"Really?"

"Really."

Seth led Natasha by the hand to the couch and continued to kiss her as he caressed her cheeks and hair. Suddenly, he reached the realization that all the waiting was over and surrendered himself to passion. He held her, reaching under her shirt and across her back to unsnap her bra. Meeting no resistance, he slipped his hand under the cup and caressed her breast. She sighed and kissed his neck.

He reached down below her undergarments, and she matched his strokes under his as they continued to kiss. At the height of passion, both of them lost control and began to strip each other, one garment at a time while they explored each other's body. As their passion gained fury, Seth perched above her, looked into her wanting eyes, and he sank into the moist and hot bed between her thighs.

CHAPTER 43

When Seth opened his eyes the next morning, the pleasant sight of Natasha's sweet sleeping face on her pillow was the first thing he saw. Her eyes opened, and they exchanged mutual smiles.

"Good morning," she said.

"The best morning."

"I'll fix breakfast."

Seth would have given anything to prolong this pleasure, but it was Monday morning, and he needed an excuse to complete his surveillance. As Natasha put freshly poached eggs and toast on the table, Seth said to her, "I probably won't go to work today."

"Why? Are you sick?"

"I'm getting a little cold, I think. Hope you don't get it."

"I'll be right over after work to take care of you."

"Really, that's not necessary."

"Nonsense. The borscht is better the second day. It'll make you feel healthy in no time."

There was no sense arguing with her. Arguing with a woman after she's made up her mind about something is as useless as taking a shower with your clothes on.

After a tasty breakfast of poached eggs and toast, Natasha left for work, and Seth took his post at the café across from Dave's apartment building and watched. After a few hours, Julia came out, turned right, and walked right past the café. He put some money on the table for his bill, followed her, and lost himself in the crowd that was moving along the street to conceal himself from her, but not so much that he was not able to see her.

When she finally reached her destination, Seth was relieved to see that it was the shopping mall. He had at least one hour – maybe an hour and a half to be safe - to get into Dave's apartment, copy his hard drive, and install the spyware. He quickly trotted back to Dave's apartment.

Seth rang the bell for Dave's apartment, just to make sure it was really empty. He waited a few moments and then rang several other neighbors' bells until he got buzzed in at random.

He went up the stairs to the first landing, inserted his homemade key into the lock, and turned it until he heard the multiple cylinders click one, two, three times – then he was inside.

Seth took a look around the apartment. It had a small corridor, a bathroom, a living room, and kitchen. The apartment was in pretty clean condition so he assumed Julia was a good housekeeper, or that she had hired one. There were two bedrooms - each with a bed, a small desk, and a laptop. Seth was surprised that they had not taken any precautions to guard against access.

One bedroom was clean and tidy. Its closet was full of women's clothes. The other was unkempt and messy. The bed was not even made. It was a double bed but only slept in on the right side. The closet in this room had only men's clothes. It was obvious that Dave and Julia did not sleep together. Seth quickly filed that thought away because there were two computers to crack instead of one like he had expected. He started on the one in the messy room.

This was Dave's laptop, and it was not easy to get past his password as it was with Bill's computer. After sweating over it for about fifteen minutes, he was in, but it was fifteen minutes that he couldn't get back. Seth loaded the spyware program, plugged in a flash drive, and started copying Dave's files. Then he went into the other room to crack Julia's computer.

Julia's password was even harder to crack. Seth checked the time. He had, at worst, half an hour and, at best, 45 minutes, and there was no way to copy the hard drives any faster. He set up his flash drive to copy Julia's documents file and went back to the other room to check on Dave's computer. The copying was 65% complete. Then he heard the cylinders turning in the lock of the front door. He pulled out the flash drive, put it in his jacket pocket, and ran into the other room, closing the door behind him as he had found it.

"Julia?"

It was Dave's voice in the corridor. Seth looked for an escape – there was none. He opened the window and looked out at the small uncovered balcony. This would have to do. He pulled the window closed as best he could and looked down. It was a one-story drop to the ground, but, if he hung from the balcony, he could cut the distance of his fall to avoid injuring himself. Just as he put his leg over the railing in order to begin his descent, he looked back into the room and saw his flash drive blinking in the USB slot of Julia's computer. *Shit.* It had already been about two minutes since Dave had entered and called Julia's name.

Seth could either risk going back into the room or leave his flash drive in her computer. He quickly reopened the window, jumped back into the room, grabbed the flash drive, and went back out, closing the window behind him. Swinging first one, then both legs over the balcony railing, Seth turned toward the window and lowered himself down on the balcony rails until he was hanging from the bottom of the balcony. He was either going to break both of his ankles and lay on the ground until someone helped him or walk away. Mustering up his courage, he let go of his grip and fell.

CHAPTER 44

"Did you really think you could get away with this?" Bill wagged the gun at the briefcase, like he was scolding Seth. "Just give me the reports, Seth."

"What reports?"

Seth's briefcase was dangling at his left side, and his right hand was on the suitcase which was teetering precariously on the edge of a step.

"Don't play dumb with me, Seth. You have no idea who you're dealing with."

"Would you really shoot me, Bill?"

"Wanna find out?"

Seth had no time to think to make the next decision, which could be one of life or death. He wasn't sure if Bill had the cold bloodedness to kill him, but he certainly had a lot to lose if Seth went public with the reports, and desperate men are known to take desperate measures. When he contemplated taking these actions, he never considered that it would get this dangerous. It was too late to turn back now because it was his life that was immediately at risk.

Seth pushed the suitcase as hard as he could at Bill which tumbled and bumped and struck him, knocking him over. Seth heard the sound of a gunshot as he turned and ran back up the stairs as fast as he could, through the parking lot and descended the staircase at the other end of the lot. He crossed the street to the ticketing area for United Airlines, all the while looking from every direction for Bill or anyone else who could be pursuing him. Coming after him personally, was a desperate measure for Bill. The good news was that it probably meant Seth was only being pur-

168

sued by Germinat and that Bill wanted to keep it quiet, if possible. That could not last for long.

Seth approached the United counter. Thank God there was no line. He paid for his ticket and headed for security. Bill would never get through there without a boarding pass and certainly not with a gun.

In the lounge, Seth sat down, hands still shaking, and put his briefcase on his lap to pull out his laptop so he could schedule his flight to Moscow as soon as possible after arriving in Washington. As he did, he saw it – the bullet had ripped a hole right through the briefcase. That was too close. A shiver went up Seth's spine. Seth always knew he was going to die – it is something we all face – but he had never come that close to it before and had never thought about it. He didn't even feel like he had lived yet.

He got out the laptop, powered it up, and booked a corresponding flight to Moscow. Then he began researching Russian media in his quest to find someone to tell his story to the public. Of course, most of the media was in the Russian language, and he wanted the coverage to be as broad as possible. He searched for western correspondents in Russia. There was the Guardian, which could make a good disclosure vehicle for the documents, except, of course, the classified report, which he intended to hold onto for as long as possible.

He would telephone the Guardian from Washington and send them a secure link to download the materials. That, no doubt, would brand Seth with another label in addition to traitor and spy – fugitive.

CHAPTER 45

Seth hit the ground hard with both feet and then fell back on his butt. The fall was painful and struck a nerve in his tailbone that seemed to ring a bell in his brain. He scrambled to get up. Everything appeared to be working, nothing broken. Standing up, he felt that his feet were in good marching order and saw that everyone around him was staring so he slipped away into the crowd of pedestrians on the sidewalk. He wanted to get as far away from Dave's building as possible. Seth checked his pockets for the hard drive and the flash drive with what had been partially downloaded from both computers. Everything was there.

When Seth got home, he quickly powered up his laptop and opened the flash drive he'd copied from Dave's computer. Dave had an impressive collection of homemade porn, some video games, and several work files. The one in particular that interested him was entitled "George Aimers."

"Subject George Aimers is a white male, approximately 6 feet tall, 190 pounds, dark-brown hair and no facial hair, brown eye color. Build matches subject Seth Rogan but cannot confirm match on other physical characteristics. Further investigation required."

It was clear to Seth that he was the subject of an investigation but unclear what that investigation was all about. Was it to capture Seth Rogan? Eliminate him? Surely, if Dave had confirmed any of his suspicions about who Seth was, he would have done that already.

"*Subject Aimers claims to be Canadian from Vancouver. Highly knowledgeable about the area. Cover identity stands up. Valid passport, but no Internet history.*"

Seth skimmed further through Dave's reports. The latest was dated just last week, after Dave's disastrous drunken night.

"*Attempt to obtain fingerprint data unsuccessful. Will continue to attempt confirmation that Subject Aimers is cover identity for Subject Rogan.*"

Dave certainly wasn't making any effort to obtain Seth's fingerprints the night they went out together. He found no clue in the 75% of Dave's hard drive that he was able to capture as to what Dave's orders were or his mission. Nowhere in Dave's files did he identify his real name or the fact that he was an FBI agent. Next, he fired up the flash drive to examine the contents of Julia's hard drive. There were folders with miscellaneous pictures (no porn like Dave's), and, surprisingly, a folder on Seth Rogan and one on George Aimers. This confirmed what Seth had suspected from the discovery that Dave and Julia were either not married, swingers, or the unhappiest married couple in the world. Julia was FBI as well.

Julia was, apparently, also a computer expert, "*Great,*" thought Seth. "*She'll probably pick up the spyware right away and will know they are under surveillance themselves.*" She had folders on Seth Rogan, detailing all of his disclosures to the press, as well as his movements into and around Moscow. She had folders on George Aimers which contained investigative reports on Aimers from various comprehensive Internet databases she had accessed and studied.

In contrast to Dave's reports, Julia was relatively certain that George Aimers and Seth Rogan were one and the same.

Subject Aimers has an American accent and, despite his attempt to disguise himself, matches the description of Seth Rogan. Leave it to a woman to notice all of the little details that men often ignore. *Request made to execute directive.* What directive? Was Seth to be assassinated? Arrested? Nothing in the materials he obtained from either computer shed any light on that ultimate question.

CHAPTER 46

Wise men throughout history are quoted for the wisdom in making friends with their enemies. Accordingly, Seth was already on that path. Natasha and Seth invited Julia and Dave over for a home-cooked meal, and they gladly accepted. In the meantime, Yuri was using the impression key borrowed from Seth to search their apartment and plant sophisticated surveillance equipment. Of course, Seth didn't confide in Yuri that he had already been in the apartment; only that he had made the key. Hopefully, Yuri would be forthcoming if he uncovered any new information.

Dinner was pleasant, and Julia and Dave proved to be good company, enforcing the notion that your worst enemy could also be your best friend. The converse had already been proven to Seth during his teenage years.

"We're going to the south of France this summer," said Julia.

"You two should go with us," said Dave.

"Sounds interesting," responded Seth.

"Have you ever been?" asked Dave.

"No."

To that, Natasha looked at Seth strangely. She had heard all of Seth's stories about the south of France and how it was one of his most favorite places and wondered why he saw the need to lie to them.

"All the more reason to go," said Dave. "I hear the parties in St. Tropez are pretty intense."

"Wouldn't know about that," said Seth.

"Do you speak French?" asked Natasha.

"Mais, oui," said Dave. "Vous parlez francais?"

"Me? No." Natasha laughed. "But George does."

"Vraiment, George?"

"Well, ya know, I am from Canada."

"You guys really have to come. France is the most romantic country in the world," said Julia.

As the night went on, Seth wondered about Yuri's progress. He figured he must be done by now. This was a high stakes game in which nobody could be trusted, and, even though Seth trusted Yuri out of necessity, and he was a great guy, he still was not sure if he would share all of his discoveries with him.

CHAPTER 47

"What did you find out?"

"They are spying on you, Seth. They can't be trusted," said Yuri.

"What do they want?"

"Whatever you have against the government. That's what they want. You should give it to me for safekeeping."

Seth trusted Yuri, but what if he were captured, tortured? *Would he give his life to protect Seth's secret? The only one who could really make that leap of faith was Seth, and only in himself.*

"I can't give it to anyone, Yuri. It's the only thing keeping me alive. I trust you, but in anyone's hands but my own, it's worthless."

"Just don't have hands on it when they come for it. They have no problem chopping off hand to get report."

"Did you find out what they have been authorized to do?"

"Only that they need to get report from you. Better reason to give to me so nobody can get it. With that report, you are a dead man."

"Exactly. What if they kill you? Once they get the report, there will be no reason to keep me alive."

Seth hoped that Yuri was not offended. If he were, he didn't show it. Yuri had been the only constant in this entire ordeal, except, of course, for Natasha, but she was not really involved in this story, only the hope of happiness that waited beyond the end of it.

After Yuri left, Seth began thinking of a new hiding place for his contraband. Carrying everything around in a briefcase, even if he kept duplicates elsewhere, was not going to insure his safety. His apartment would be searched. He would be searched. Eventually, they would find the report, and his life insurance policy would have expired. There had to be a place that was safe. He trudged all over the apartment, looking in every nook and cranny for a possible hiding place. Unfortunately, too many of them were cliché, and he had already had experience with his apartment being ransacked.

Eventually, he settled on taking the cover off the electrical outlet. He unplugged the lamp and took off the cover. There was just enough space there in the wall to the side of the electrical outlet to hide the disk and the report if he rolled it up. He rolled the report, tucked the valuables in the spot, screwed the cover back on, and plugged the lamp back in. The rest was up to fate.

CHAPTER 48

Seth was restless in anticipation of his dinner date with Natasha. With all the "covert operations" that had been going on, they had hardly had any time together. The taxi dispatcher called and told Seth the taxi he ordered was a white taxi with the numbers 234. Seth's Russian was good enough, at this point, to order a taxi and get around the town without feeling like a complete fool. He looked at the window and saw the taxi waiting so he quickly put on his boots, coat and hat, and went out.

Seth opened the door and was surprised to find a man in the back seat and one in the front passenger seat, both dressed in suits, and both looked very American.

"Sorry, I thought this was my taxi," he said to the driver in Russian.

"It is your taxi. Get in," said the man in the back seat in perfect English with an American accent. He had cold, steel-gray eyes and looked very serious.

"We just want to talk to you," he said.

Seth followed his first instinct, which was to turn and run back into the apartment, and, as he did, another suited man stood face-to-face with him and said, "Get in the car, please." Seth reluctantly sat down in between the two men in the back. The gray-eyed man did all the talking.

"We will drop you off at your destination. We just need to talk," said Grey Eyes.

The taxi slowly pulled away.

"What would you like to talk about?"

"We know who you are," said the man.

"That puts me at somewhat of a disadvantage because I don't know who you are," said Seth.

"You don't need to know who we are, only what we can offer you."

" What would that be?"

"Safe passage back to the United States, and the guarantee of a fair deal," said Grey Eyes.

"Why should I trust you?"

"Who do you think you should trust, Dave Salisbury?"

"What about him?"

"We know he's FBI. You're really better off with us."

"Why is that?"

"Because we can keep you alive. That is your primary concern, is it not?"

"What is it that you want?"

"You know what we want."

"Well, maybe I do and maybe I don't. Why don't you humor me by spelling it out?"

"The classified report."

"You're assuming I have this report...." Grey Eyes interrupted Seth.

"We know you have it," he said.

"I don't know how you came about that information because, presently, I do not have it, but, if I did, since I don't know who you are, how would I feel comfortable giving it to you?"

"We represent the United States government," said Grey Eyes.

"So does Dave Salisbury," said Seth.

"Yes, but he is operating outside the scope of his authority."

Seth didn't know why Salisbury was dogging him, but he needed some kind of leverage.

"What makes you think that your deal is any better than the deal that Salisbury offered to me?"

"He didn't offer you any deal," said Grey Eyes.

"Oh, but he did." That raised Grey Eyes' eyebrows.

" He can't guarantee your safety. Only we can."

"How do you know that since I don't even know you work for the government? You haven't even shown me any ID."

"Salisbury didn't give you any either."

"On the contrary, he presented me with his FBI identification," said Seth.

"What are you talking about? You don't even know his real name."

"Brian Jenkins," said Seth.

This surprised all three G-Men, and Grey Eyes seemed a little taken aback, like he had just taken a bite of a hot chili pepper.

"Then are we to assume that you have accepted his offer?"

"I haven't decided. What makes you think that your offer would be more palatable to me?"

"Mr. Jenkins cannot keep you safe," said Grey Eyes. "Listen carefully because we are not going to negotiate this. Get the report and all copies of it, and meet us in the lobby of the Parus Hotel tomorrow at 8 p.m. Come alone."

"If I don't show up?

"The consequences of non-compliance will be met with strict enforcement action. You do know about shock and awe, don't you?"

Seth was all too familiar with the trigger happy antics of the current government, and the consequences did not require any further information.

The taxi pulled up to the restaurant and stopped. The man next to Seth got out, and Seth exited after him. As quickly as they had appeared, they were gone.

CHAPTER 49

All through dinner with Natasha, Seth was not at ease. He glanced around nervously, looking at the entrance and the kitchen door.

"Seth, what's wrong?" asked Natasha.

"Nothing, really, I guess I've just been a little jumpy lately."

"I'll say you are. Calm down. Relax."

"I'm fine."

After finishing dinner, Seth was still uneasy. He excused himself to go the restroom, and there he flipped out his cell phone and called Yuri.

"Yuri, I was ambushed by three guys tonight."

"I know."

"You know? You let them get me?"

"CIA Seth. Remember I told you not to go out of town? First, they sent Salisbury and now they sent these guys. They aren't going to mess around. Their first visit is always where they give the ultimatum. You don't want second visit. Believe me. We have to take measures."

"What measures?"

"Let's talk about that in person. I meet you at apartment in one hour."

CHAPTER 50

When Seth got back to the apartment, the door was ajar and looked like it had been jimmied open. The door frame was bent. He called Yuri on the cell phone.

"I'm on my way," said Yuri. "Don't go in until I get there."

Seth trusted Yuri, but he had to check and make sure his hiding place had not been touched. If the report had already fallen into the wrong hands, he was as good as dead."

He looked through the crack of the half-opened door and listened for any sounds of movement. It was as still inside as a meadow at midnight. He carefully slipped in, remembering the time his apartment in St. Louis had been ransacked. This time nobody struck him on the head – yet.

What greeted Seth was what was becoming too familiar of a scene. Food was dumped all over the kitchen floor, the contents of the refrigerator mixed with spices, pasta, rice, cereal and broken glass. Every drawer was stretched out like a tongue at a doctor's office. Every cabinet door was gaping open. All the contents of Seth's entire apartment now covered the floor like a badly sewn quilt. Thank God, the cover plate was intact. Seth reached into his pocket for his keys to unscrew the plate, and, as he bent over to do it, Yuri walked in, and Seth immediately stopped.

"What you are doing? I thought I told you to wait outside," he admonished.

"Uh, just looking around."

"Did they get it?"

"What?"

"What they were looking for. Did they get it?"

"No, no, it's not, it's not even here."

"Where is it? You can't fuck around anymore. This is only thing between you and cut throat. You have to give it to me for safekeeping, or you are as good as dead."

"I told you. It's not here. It's safe."

"Safe?"

Seth looked around at the torn cushions of the couch and stuffing all over the living room. He knew Yuri was right.

"Yes."

"Look, Seth, we already know your shitty skills as a spy. You got three CIA guys after you. What they say to you?"

"To give them the report, and I will be safe."

"We have to get you out of here right away. First thing you need to do is to give me report. Stop fucking around. By tomorrow, you have to be ten thousand kilometers from here."

"I think we should talk to Dave first."

"Talk to Dave? Are you out of your mind?"

"Look, if Dave were supposed to get me, then why would these guys be after me? I think they're working two different sides."

"What, I duck your head into car for high speed chase and gun battle, and now you think you are expert detective? Man, you are way, way out of your league."

"Maybe so, but it's logical."

"Seth, for smart guy, sometimes you can be so fucking stupid. There is no logical in spy business. Instincts defy logic. You have to be quick or you are dead. There is always some guy out there who is quicker than you. The only logic is how not to meet that quicker guy."

Seth knew Yuri was right, but he had to talk to Dave first. It was the only piece of the puzzle that did not fit. Neither Dave nor Julia had threatened him or asked him for the report. He knew the CIA's agenda. He knew he didn't dare meet with them, and he knew he needed Yuri's protection. He had to find out what Dave was doing.

"Come on. You go to hotel tonight. Not safe here."

Seth saw his briefcase on the floor among the debris, open and empty, of course. He picked it up and closed it.

"Yuri, I...Okay, let me get some stuff."

"Seth, you know there is cat and there is mouse, right?"

"Yes."

"Mouse smells piece of cheese, he runs to it, bites into it without looking and BAM! - he is smashed to pieces by mousetrap. But cat is different. Cat sees mouse and becomes very, very still. He looks at every move of mouse, creeps up on mouse without mouse seeing him and is very, very patient. Cat crouches low and stays there like statue, as long as it takes. Every one of cat's muscles is tensed, ready to strike at the right moment, and cat waits until that very moment, then BAM! - mouse is in cat's claws. Mouse never saw him coming."

"And?"

"Simple. Be cat, not mouse. Cat lives longer."

CHAPTER 51

Seth kept rolling around in the little hotel bed. He couldn't possibly sleep. He kept thinking, staring up at the ceiling, then closing his eyes to try to force himself to sleep. He turned to one side, then the other side. It seemed like every part of his body itched. He scratched, then turned over again. Ridiculous lyrics to the same song, *Heard it through the Grapevine*, bounced around in his brain, refusing to be evicted. Finally, he called Dave.

"Dave, it's George."

"George, how are you?"

"I'm good – look, I'm sorry it's late, but we have to talk."

"George, I'm not much of a phone guy. If you want to get together, let's get together, and we can talk then."

"When?"

"Well, how about right now?"

"Okay. Where?"

"Remember that hotel we went to with those two chicks. Just say yes or no."

"Yes."

"Meet me there."

"Okay."

"Be careful Seth. It's late and there are a lot of lowlifes out there. Don't trust anyone at this time of night."

The phone went dead. Seth looked out the grimy window of his tiny room. He thought he understood Dave's cryptic code speech. If he tried to walk there, he would freeze after a few long blocks. If he called a taxi, he may have uninvited company again. He decided to slip out and hail a cab on the street.

Seth went by the cloak room in the lobby bar, and grabbed a stranger's coat and hat from the coat rack. He waited for a couple of drunks to leave, then staggered out the front entrance with them, slushing his boots randomly through the snow, and followed the drunks into a mini-mart where they bought cigarettes and some beers for the road. Seth bought a pack of cigarettes and some matches and exited the mini-mart, lighting one. A taxi was waiting outside the mini-mart, and Seth asked the driver in Russian if he were free. He hopped in the cab and was whisked within a block of Hollywood Palace, then got out and walked the rest of the way on foot.

Dave was waiting in the same suite. Seth knocked on the door, and Dave opened it. As Seth entered the suite, he could see that Dave was not alone. Julia was also there.

"Have a seat, George," said Dave

"Thanks."

Seth sat in one of the two chairs opposite the large couch with Dave on the left side, closest to him, and Julia on the right.

"Who else knows you're here?"

"Nobody."

"Were you followed?"

"No. I took precautions."

"Good."

"Dave, I was confronted tonight by three American guys."

"CIA. We knew they were in town."

"Yes, and they made me an offer."

"What did they offer you?"

"Before that, I'd like to know your offer."

"My offer?"

"Yes."

Seth looked over at Julia sitting on the couch. She seemed to be trying to read his mind. She scooted closer, opposite Seth.

"We came here to Russia as a result of your request," said Julia.

"My request?"

"Yes, you said you wanted a Congressional investigation. Several members of the Senate are in agreement with you. These are very powerful people, with very specific requirements."

"Before we get into their requirements, what are they offering to me?"

"We're here on their behalf because you said you wanted an investigation," said Dave. "That means, if you accept, you testify before Senate hearings, and you receive immunity for your testimony as long as you turn over all classified information to the Committee and let them deal with it as they see fit."

"This means all copies of everything you have," said Julia. "Anything shows up on the street or in the press and there is no deal. No immunity."

"What about the other stuff? The FDA and EPA reports about GMO food?"

"The Senate hearing is about government corruption. Since you've already made those reports public, they are known, but they still have to be presented to the Committee."

" How do I know I can trust you?"

"You have no choice," said Julia. "The CIA has made an appointment with you to deliver the report, right?"

"Right."

"If you don't make the appointment, they will come after you. I think you know that you are in better hands with us, or you wouldn't be here."

"When is the appointment?" asked Dave.

"Tomorrow. Eight o'clock. Look, the FSB has also been asking me for the report."

"George," said Dave. "Are you American or Russian?"

"Well, actually I'm Canadian right now."

"Right, sure you are. Well, you can't turn over this information to the Russians. First of all, it does you no good. It won't get you any closer to a Congressional investigation, and isn't this why you put your ass into hot water in the first place? To try to change things?"

"Well, yes..."

"Second, you cannot trust anybody – even your protectors."

"Technically, that includes you, Dave."

"Fair enough, but the fact that you're here and have not turned over the report to the Russians says that you have already made your decision. Is the report safe?"

"Yes."

"You have it hidden somewhere?"

"Yes."

"The best bet is to get it while the CIA is waiting for you. Less chance for them to track you when they're sitting there for the appointment. Let's meet, secure the report, then get you out of Russia as soon as possible."

"Then what?"

"You'll travel to the states on your Canadian passport," said Julia. "U.S. Marshals will pick you up at the border and take you to a safe house. You will be enrolled in the witness protection program for your safety. That means a new identity, a new location."

"How do I know this isn't all bullshit?" asked Seth.

"We put the deal in writing," said Dave, as he lifted his briefcase onto his lap, opened it, and took out some papers. Dave slid the papers to Seth on the coffee table."

"This is the best deal you will ever make," Julia said.

Seth read over the papers. They were from the U.S. Attorney's Office, they looked official, and seemed to provide everything Dave said they would.

"Because it's a government corruption case, you can rest assured that nobody in the government, except for the U.S. Marshal, will know who you are or where you are," said Dave.

"Would I be able to bring my girlfriend with me?" asked Seth.

"If you were married, the deal would cover both parties," said Julia. "If not, I'm afraid they wouldn't even be able to tell her where you are."

Seth thought hard about this. If he signed the deal, he wouldn't be able to see Natasha for some time, maybe a long time. If he didn't sign the deal, he would surely be killed or thrown into an obscure prison. If they could find him in Russia, they could find him anywhere. He needed to tap the same kind of unlimited government resources to hide as they had used to find him. He signed the deal.

"You made the right decision," said Dave.

Now if only he could live long enough to see it through.

CHAPTER 52

Seth woke after a restless sleep and a series of strange dreams. He called Natasha.

"Natasha, would you mind taking the class today?"

"Sure, what's going on?"

"I've got some important business to take care of."

"George, what kind of business could you have in Russia?"

"It's complicated, and I really can't explain it now, but I promise, I'll explain it to you later. The most important thing is that I want you to know that meeting you has been the brightest point of my life, and I don't want to lose what we have."

"We won't."

"If anything happens, just remember that."

"What do you mean?"

"Life gets complicated. Sometimes there are things you just can't control. Just know that I am always thinking of you and that we will be together, I promise."

"Sounds like a good-bye. What's happening?"

"I'll tell you everything. I just can't right now."

"George, you're scaring me."

"Sorry, I don't mean to. I'll call you later today, okay?"

Time was passing too quickly toward eight o'clock. By seven-thirty, Dave and Seth would be at the apartment. By eight, they and Julia would be on their way to a safe house near the airport. By nine the next morning, they would be on a flight to Moscow.

At seven-twenty, Seth was out the door and walking toward the mini-mart. Dave was waiting for him there in his car. They drove to Seth's apartment, securing the car in the garage area a short walk from the building. The building looked quiet. Nobody was going in, out or hanging around. There didn't seem to be anyone watching the perimeter. Dave picked up a black bag from the back seat as they both exited the car.

"What's that for?" asked Seth.

"My bag of tricks. You never know."

The apartment door was no longer open. In fact, the door had been replaced. Seth tried to open it, and it was locked. He tried his key in the lock, but it didn't work.

"The lock's been changed," said Seth.

"Stand back."

Dave pulled a heavy-duty crowbar out of the black bag, wedged it in the door jamb, and popped the door open with one easy movement.

The apartment was still in a state of disarray. "Don't turn on the lights," said Dave, handing Seth a flashlight.

Seth turned on the flashlight, and they entered the living room without taking off their coats and boots. They were not staying.

Seth shined the light on the cover plate and unscrewed it. The printout of the report and flash drive were still there. He pulled them out, then stood up to give them to Dave.

"I've got them," he said.

Seth heard a loud "POP" and saw Dave crumple to his knees, and then fall on his bag. He shined the light on Dave and saw his coat soaked up with blood. There was blood coming from the corner of Dave's mouth. Seth panicked. The CIA must have ambushed them. He crouched down and shined the light toward the door.

Then he heard a familiar voice say, "I will take that, Seth." The lights flipped on and there was Yuri, standing in the corridor, holding his pistol, trained right at Seth. Dave was choking, still alive. Yuri pointed the gun at his head and fired, blasting particles of Dave's brain all over the floor and wall. Seth, terrified, jumped, and started to gag.

"I told you so many times, Seth. You are shitty spy."

"Why are you doing this?"

"Simple. Your guys pay more. Now give me report."

"If I give it to you, you'll let me go?"

"No, but, if you don't give it to me, I shoot you and take it."

"You're going to shoot me anyway."

"Right. Seth, I like you, but this is business. Spy business is dirty business."

"What about Dave?"

"Fugitive kills FBI agent. I was watching apartment and heard gunshot. When I came in, FBI agent was dead, and you were holding stolen gun in hand, pointed at me. I shot you to defend myself. Now hand over report, and I promise I will not make you suffer. One shot to head. You won't feel nothing."

Yuri moved his gun in a "come here" manner, beckoning Seth to turn over the report.

"Come on Seth. Time's up."

Seth stood there, frozen, unable to move. Suddenly, he heard the crack of four rapidly fired gunshots, and Yuri fell to the floor, his gun clattering out in front of him. Behind him, standing in the ready firing position, was Natasha, with hand outstretched. In her hand, was a pistol. Smoke poured from the barrel like the wisp of smoke that emanates from a cigarette after a long drag. Her firing hand was shaking.

Seth was in shock but pumped with adrenalin. He quickly kicked Yuri's gun out of the way, across the floor. Judging from the blood pooling around his torso, he was in no position to use it. Natasha was crying now. Seth embraced her, and she fell into him.

"I've never killed anyone," she said, sobbing.

"You'll be okay. We have to leave now. Do you have a car?"

"No."

"Watch the door."

Seth fumbled through Dave's coat pockets for his car keys, found them, and put them in his pocket, along with the report and the flash drive. He ushered Natasha out. She was still shaking.

"What on earth were you doing there and with a gun? You saved my life."

"I'm FSB."

"What?"

"I was assigned to you as backup. Yuri never knew of my existence."

"Then, everything between us - that was all just part of your cover?"

"No George – Seth - everything between us was real, I swear. I didn't count on falling in love with you."

"You're in love with me?"

"I didn't want to tell you this way." Natasha's face was pained. She was suffering.

"I was going to tell you, but it was just too dangerous. I have a deal with the FBI. We need to get to Julia right away."

"First, I have to call this in."

Seth could see that her hands were still shaking as she took out her cell phone and called in the crime scene. She spoke on the phone for several minutes. After the call, she was controlled but still visibly upset.

"I have to tell you what is going to happen," she said, as she put away the cell phone. "An FBI agent is dead at the hands of one of our FSB agents who went rogue. The Americans will deny that he was working for their own CIA. This cannot be an international incident. Yuri's body will be removed from the scene, and Dave's death will be deemed an unsolved matter with no suspects. They can't promise how the Americans will react, but the FSB was officially never here."

"I understand. What about me?"

"The Americans will probably want to name you as a primary suspect, but, as far as our investigation is concerned, since I was a witness, you are in the clear in Russia. Since they will probably be after Seth Rogan as well as George Aimers, you'll be given a new passport and immigration papers. You can probably forget about the asylum application."

"Julia can clear all this up. I signed a deal with the U.S. Attorney for immunity for my testimony before a Congressional investigation. She has it."

"Yes, she is your best way to get out of this mess. We have to get rid of those three CIA agents."

"Get rid of them? You mean kill them?"

"No, of course not. We just have to get enough information from them to prove they have violated the terms of their visa, and they will be asked to leave."

They walked carefully, slowly, and methodically to Dave's car with Seth leading the way.

"I'll drive. I know the roads better," said Natasha.

They got in, and Natasha pulled out, turning right onto the street. As they approached Dave's building, they could see police cars parked outside of it. They parked Dave's car in the back and used his security key to get in the building.

When they got in the building, Dave's door was open. They were stopped at the entrance by a uniformed police officer. Natasha showed her FSB badge, and they went inside. Two other uniformed officers and what appeared to be a police detective in civilian attire were gathered around the lifeless body of Julia, which was surrounded by a pool of fresh blood. Natasha talked to the officers.

"There are no papers here. Nothing. The computers have been taken as well."

Seth now was not only probably the only suspect in the murder of two FBI agents, but he no longer had a deal with the FBI. That deal had died with Dave and Julia.

CHAPTER 53

The next task was to deal with the three CIA agents waiting for Seth in the lobby of the Parus Hotel. Natasha called for backup as they made their way to the meeting.

The Parus was an elegant, European-style hotel, built inside a late 19th century mansion that must have been home to one of the first Far East noble families. They made their way to the lovely grand entrance where Natasha spotted her backup – three FSB agents dressed like gardeners or groundsmen, one dressed as a doorman, and three others dressed like business-men. One of the "gardeners" took them aside and equipped Seth with a wire for his meeting.

As they entered the lobby, the "businessmen" followed them. Natasha and the "businessmen" took a seat at a nearby table while Seth approached the three nameless agents.

"Good evening, Mr. Rogan," said the gray-eyed agent.

"Good evening."

"You're late. We almost gave up on you."

"Something came up."

"Well, let's get down to business, shall we?" the agent said, as he lit a cigarette, without bothering to ask Seth if he minded the smoking. "You have something we need, and we have some-thing that may be of interest to you."

"What's that?" Seth spurted out, wryly.

Grey Eyes looked surprised at Seth's newfound boldness.

"I thought you valued your freedom," said the agent.

" Are you in any position to take it away?"

"The United States government does not take lightly to having its secrets being stolen by its contractors, Mr. Rogan. I can assure you that, if you do not cooperate with us, we cannot guarantee your safety inside or outside of Russia."

"Are you threatening me?"

"Not threatening – educating."

"I don't see that you gentlemen are here in any official capacity. Are you?"

"What do you mean?"

"I mean, does the Russian government just let CIA agents wander around, threatening people under their protection? Is that a norm for them?"

"The Russians cannot protect you from the wrath of the United States."

"Who dispenses that wrath – you?"

"Look, Rogan, don't fuck with the CIA. Like I told you before, we don't negotiate. Now give the fucking report to me if you want to live." Grey Eyes pulled back the corner of his jacket, revealing a weapon tucked under his belt.

With that, Natasha and her three businessmen, as well as the doorman, approached the agents at gunpoint. Natasha flashed her badge to them and smiled.

"FSB gentlemen. Please put your hands on your heads." The three businessmen frisked the agents, removing their weapons.

"May I see your passports please?" Natasha said, politely. "Were you aware that handguns are forbidden in Russia?"

The three agents did not expect this. Obviously, they had made their deal with Yuri, and he had done his part. They had no idea that Seth had a backup. They turned out to be holding visitors' visas and had no official business in Russia. Plus, they were in possession of firearms without permits. Natasha left them in the capable hands of the three businessmen and the doorman, and they left, giving Seth's wire to the "gardeners" as they exited.

"What will happen to them now?"

"Their visas will be revoked, and they will be invited to leave the country."

"With no prosecution?"

"This would be an embarrassment for both countries. For the U.S., to have their spies caught in a criminal conspiracy, and, even worse, for Russia to have one of their own not only becoming a double agent but murdering two FBI agents. I'm afraid none of this can ever come to light."

"What do we do now?"

"We relocate until you can make your next move."

CHAPTER 54

Seth's last hope – Julia – had been eliminated. He wasn't sure if it were the CIA agents or Yuri who had done it, but, either way, she was just as dead. Seth waited in the lobby of the local FSB office, a front disguised as a travel agency, while Natasha was picking up his new passport and paperwork, contemplating his next move. Technically, he had a deal with the FBI, but how could he get to them? Seth Rogan, aka George Aimers, was all over the Western news. Even the Russian news was reporting it. In the lobby, a television set on the news channel broadcast his picture while a foreign correspondent told the story, dubbed over in Russian.

"Seth Rogan, also known as George Aimers, the fugitive wanted for violation of the Espionage Act, is now the sole suspect in the murder of undercover FBI agents Brian Jenkins and Melissa Standing. He is still at large and presumed to be armed and dangerous. Anyone with information as to the whereabouts of Mr. Rogan is urged to call the local law enforcement office."

According to Natasha, Interpol also had an all-points bulletin out for his apprehension. They decided that Russia was the only place safe for him now. They were to make it to a safe house in St. Petersburg and lay low there until a point of contact could be made with the FBI.

The adrenalin pumping through Seth's body didn't allow him to be tired at all, but he supposed his system would come crashing down once they finally came to a place where they could rest. They made their way to a hotel near the airport and checked in.

For once in this entire ordeal, Seth was with someone he could trust with his entire story so he told the story to Natasha that night. There were no longer any secrets between them.

"Sounds like you have more spy experience than me ," she said.

"You know, I never pictured you as a spy. How did that happen?"

"Hard to say, really. My education is for teaching, but the pay is not very good, and I wanted a job where I could travel and have some excitement."

"It's quite a contrast."

"To tell you the truth, it's terrifying. After this shooting, I don't think I want to renew my contract."

"What will you do?"

"I don't know. I guess I'm in the same boat as you." A boat with a leak patched up with duct tape, a blown out motor, a hole in the sail, and no oars. It wasn't likely that Seth's application for asylum would be granted now so his time in Russia was limited to the one-year expiration of his visa. He had a few months to clear this up or disappear someplace else. It would be tough to find a country who would take not only a traitor but also one suspected of murdering two FBI agents. That was going to be a hard sell. He had to try to connect with the FBI. The paperwork had the name of the Assistant U.S. Attorney who drafted the deal. He would call him from St. Petersburg.

Natasha was too rattled from the shooting to sleep, and tossed and turned the entire night. Seth finally was able to get a few hours before they woke up to catch the early morning flight.

CHAPTER 55

St. Petersburg was about as cold as Khabarovsk, but its scenery was a festival for the senses. Many have referred to it as the "Paris of Russia." It's true that the architecture was uniquely European, but the streets were bigger, the buildings more massive, and the city was connected by a series of small canals. At night, the city glistened and glowed with lights, like a movie set made up for a night scene. Seth and Natasha shared an apartment in the center of town.

Once they settled in, Seth called the Assistant U.S. Attorney, Henry Meyers, from his Skype line. Skype takes the position that they are not a telephone company. Therefore, conversations are less likely to be tapped. Also, when Seth called from his Skype number, the caller ID on the receiving end showed a number registered in the country of the person receiving the call. His whereabouts were virtually untraceable from the call.

"Mr. Meyers, this is Seth Rogan."

"Mr. Rogan, you're a wanted man. If you called to turn yourself in, I'm afraid you've called the wrong person."

"No, Mr. Meyers, I want to speak to you. I intend to turn myself in, but only to the FBI and only on condition that you honor the deal that I signed."

"That may be a little difficult, given the fact that you killed the two agents who brought you the deal."

"I didn't kill anyone."

"Well, Mr. Rogan, I'm not the judge or jury here. Can you at least tell me where you are?"

"Not yet."

"Well, then I guess we have nothing to talk about."

"Wait – are you still interested in the Congressional investigation of the FDA and the EPA?"

"Yes, but..."

"Am I your primary witness?"

"Yes."

"Well, then I don't see that you have much of a choice."

"A witness who killed two FBI agents does not make a very credible one, does he?"

"No, but you know as well as I do that the charge is bullshit, and that there is no evidence against me. It was put there by the same people who don't want me to testify."

"Mr. Rogan, assuming this is true, how do you intend to prove that?"

"I thought I was presumed innocent until proven guilty beyond a reasonable doubt."

"Yes, that is true."

"If there is no evidence against me, an indictment will not issue."

"Also true, but..."

"Why don't you convene a grand jury for my indictment? When they fail to indict, I can surrender myself to the FBI and we can go through with the deal."

"Mr. Rogan, are you a scientist or an attorney? What stops you from coming in now?"

"If I am held or charged with being a terrorist and turn myself in, do you think anyone will ever see me, let alone the Committee?"

Seth knew that the bogus arrest warrant was there for only one reason – to capture him and prevent him from testifying at the Congressional hearing.

"I see your point. I'll get back to you."

CHAPTER 56

The days and nights spent with Natasha in St. Petersburg almost made Seth forget that precious time was passing and this would all soon come to an end. Russians lived each day as if it were their last, and this is how Seth chose to live this time. Every minute, which turned into hours, which turned into days, and then into nights, was special. There was no ordinary full moon, no ordinary sunset; not then and not ever again.

It seemed like there were only two seasons in Russia – winter and summer – but, even though it was still cold, the signs of spring were appearing. You could feel it, even smell it in the air, and it was almost as if you could see the trees waking up from their long winter slumber. Soon the ground, which was now a combination of mud and frost, would be carpeted with green, and new life would pop up everywhere.

It was a long and welcome break from the house of horrors they had left behind in the Far East, but there was still work to be done. Seth called Henry Meyers regularly to see if there were any news. So far, there was no news and nothing to do but wait.

At first, they spent their time holed up in the little apartment, day after day, until it seemed safe to venture outside. Natasha was the only one who left the apartment for supplies, and Seth worked on his memoirs while she was gone. During this time, they became closer and closer.

By summer, it was safe to venture out. They spent their days anonymously, going to the theater, getting lost among the priceless works of art in the vast Hermitage Museum, and walking along the streets and canals in what became the perpetual twilight in this "abstract and intentional" city of Peter the

Great and Pushkin. Seth loved every moment and never wanted to leave St. Petersburg, but everything has an end.

Just when it seemed as if it would never happen, one morning Meyers called on their secure cell phone line.

"Mr. Rogan, I think we are about ready," he said.

"What's next?"

"You will meet our man in Minsk. He has your agreement and instructions to get you safely to the U.S. Your FSB liaison will be briefed on all the details."

Seth and Natasha's days in St. Petersburg would officially come to an end the next day.

CHAPTER 57

Seth and Natasha boarded the train to Minsk at 7 p.m. Seth was saddened to say good-bye to St. Petersburg, home already to many memories, and the only home that he and Natasha had known together. By the next morning, they would arrive in Minsk where they would meet with a member of the FBI who would have a new agreement for Seth to sign. He would arrange for safe passage to the United States where Seth would be taken into the witness protection program. Natasha, who already had a U.S. visa, would join him later.

There was a lot of nothing between St. Petersburg and Belarus and, thanks to the white nights, plenty of daylight to see it all. Seth and Natasha relaxed in their private car, dining on picnic lunches that she had packed for them and sipping on tea, courtesy of the built-in samovar on board. It was very warm in the still air during stops, but, while the train was moving, there was a nice breeze.

There was nothing to do on the train except talk or play games. Some of the other passengers were playing card games or watching DVDs. Seth and Natasha knew that their time together was coming to an end, at least for a while, and the melancholy of that realization thickened the air.

"Do you think you'll stay in this profession?" he asked her.

"I don't know. I don't think it suits me."

"I thought it was usually something like a calling, you know, something you knew you just had to do."

"I guess it is for most people, but, for me, it was just an option proposed to me that I decided to accept. I knew I would be in the field, but I never thought I would have to use my weapon, let alone kill someone with it."

"Still, I'm glad they taught you how to use it."

They were to be met at the station by Natasha's Belarussian FSB counterparts. From there, Seth would be escorted to a meeting with the FBI contact for Henry Meyers.

As night fell, they sat together on the bottom bunk and held each other. It felt good, and they had no idea how long it would be before they would have the chance to be this close again.

"We should get some sleep," said Natasha.

"Too nervous to sleep."

"I know, but, if you don't, you will lose your edge. Tomorrow is a big day."

"You're right."

Seth took the top bunk. They were just big enough to barely fit one person. He stared at the ceiling, trying to clear his brain of all thoughts. Otherwise, sleep would be impossible. The rhythm of the train rumbling through the countryside was soothing and finally rocked him to sleep.

CHAPTER 58

About 30 minutes before the train arrived in Minsk, the female purser knocked on their door to announce the impending arrival. Seth and Natasha woke up and gathered their small suitcases. Seth clung to his precious briefcase. There was one copy of the report and the flash drive in it and a duplicate flash drive and report in the secret compartment of his jacket. Natasha took out and put on her body armor, then strapped on her holster, and checked the magazine for her gun.

"What are you doing?" asked Seth.

"Just getting ready," she said.

"I thought we were being met by Belarussian FSB."

"We are, but you always have to be ready for any contingency. It's a dangerous world, and this is a dangerous business."

He knew she was right, but he didn't have to like it. The thought of her facing danger again was excruciating. He had to think of a way to prevent it.

"I don't want you to get hurt."

"Seth, it's my job."

"You're here because of me. There has to be a way to keep you out of it."

"I won't leave you. We're in this together. If you're facing danger, we face it together."

The train pulled into the station and stopped, and the passengers began to shuffle out.

CHAPTER 59

Natasha and Seth waited at the door to the train so she could survey the layout before them.

"I don't like this," she said, looking out.

"Why?"

"There should be a group waiting for us. Look out there – nobody. See those two guys on the roof of the station? They could be just looking out for us, but it looks like a trap to me."

"What do we do?"

"They'll be expecting us to come out of the train and into the station. We'll just jump out the other side and walk back on the tracks. Once we're out of range, I'll call this in and find out what our next move should be."

They both slipped out the back exit and walked to the end of the train, using it as cover. When they had cleared the train, they continued down the tracks until they found a place to exit into the city. There was a small café there that would be a good place to make the call. Natasha flipped out her phone.

"Belarussian authorities got a phony call, telling them the deal was off," she said. "We have to make our way to their headquarters."

Using the directions sent to her on her cell phone, Natasha and Seth hailed a jitney driver.

The jitney driver was either too stupid or indifferent to drop them off in front of the building, instead opting for a spot across the street, leaving them exposed for the street crossing to the agency headquarters. As they made their way to the corner to cross, a man in a brown trench coat stepped out in front of them. By the time Seth noticed he was blocking their way, he also noticed that he had his gun pointed at Natasha, and she had hers pointed at him.

"Mr. Rogan, if you want your pretty little girlfriend to live, come with me," said the man.

"Don't do it," said Natasha.

"Don't hurt her," Seth said.

There was no time to think his way out of this one. If it were going to be either Natasha or him, it was going to be him.

"I'll come with you, but you have to let her go," said Seth.

The two guns still faced each other; the standoff was still on.

"Seth, step behind me," said Natasha, without taking her eye off the man in the trench coat.

"No, I'll turn myself in," said Seth, "but only if you put your gun down."

"Only if she puts hers down ," said the man.

"Forget it," said Natasha.

"Here's what I'm going to do," said Seth. "I will inch forward, one step at a time, until I am in between you and her, and then you can arrest me. Okay?"

"Okay, but make it slow."

"Seth, what are you doing?" asked a startled Natasha.

"I'm going to let him take me. At the same time, I want you to move to a position of safety," said Seth. "Once I am in front of him, you take cover."

Seth sidestepped, very slowly, inching toward the man until he was standing in front of him with the gun of the man less than two feet in front of his face."

"Run, Natasha!"

Natasha rolled to cover behind the alley wall, then stood up, training her gun on the agent, but there was no way to shoot without the risk of hitting Seth.

Once Natasha was out of harm's way, Seth quickly moved his head out of the way of the gun. At the same time, he grabbed the barrel and rotated it with his right hand and struck the man's wrist hard with his other hand. Seth played out each step as he had rehearsed it with Yuri, and it all seemed to happen in slow motion. He twisted the man's trigger finger with the barrel and heard it snap as he screamed out in pain. He kept pressure on the man's injured finger, rotated, put all his power into pushing the man to the ground. Then he pulled the gun away and pinned the man's good arm down with his foot and pointed the gun at his head. Natasha was there, her gun trained on the man, and her free hand on her cell phone calling for backup.

CHAPTER 60

Seth sat at the table in the Congressional hearing, being grilled by Senators who were obviously pro-GMO foods and those who were obviously against it. The hearings were being televised on C-SPAN. He had been supplied with Jay Standing, an attorney who sat by his side, but the rest of the audience was composed of elected officials. There were two things you could tell about a politician; the old adage about, when his lips were moving, he was probably lying and that he never spoke for himself, only for the one whose ass he happened to be kissing at the time.

"The Chair recognizes the distinguished Senator from Missouri," said the Chairman.

"Mr. Rogan, I understand that you petitioned the Russian government for political asylum. Is that correct?"

"Yes."

"Do you intend to exercise your Fifth Amendment privilege against self-incrimination?" asked the Senator.

"Objection," said Standing. "My client has an agreement of immunity with the government."

"Whatever piece of paper he has from an Assistant U.S. Attorney is not going to help him here."

"Don't respond," Standing whispered to him.

"No, I won't stay quiet on this," said Seth, and stood up.

"Senator, I don't need to exercise the Fifth Amendment because I have done nothing wrong," he said.

"Now you've done it," said his attorney. "You've opened the door."

"You say you've done nothing wrong. You stole secret government reports, sir, then fled the country" said the Senator.

"I took reports from my boss that he and the EPA were hiding from the U.S. government, and I delivered them to the FBI," said Seth.

The Chairman pounded his gavel. "That will be enough, Mr. Rogan." Seth ignored him and continued over his voice.

"I left the country because he tried to kill me to stop me from turning over the reports to the FBI."

"Order!" The Chairman pounded his gavel furiously.

"After I left the country, the CIA tried to kill me."

"That will be all, Mr. Rogan!"

"It's not all, Mr. Chairman."

"This is a Senate hearing, Mr. Rogan, and you must obey the rules of order."

"When I left, Mr. Chairman, I had the constitutional right to freedom of speech. Has that right been stripped from the American people while I was gone?"

"Mr. Rogan, you are out of order. The distinguished Senator from Missouri has the floor."

"Mr. Rogan," said the Senator, "You did break into the EPA Chief's office. Did you not?"

"Objection!" said Standing.

"He was not the EPA Chief then, Senator, he was a vice president of Germinat."

"You did break into his office. Is that correct?"

"Yes."

"You're still claiming you did nothing wrong?"

"Objection, Mr. Chairman, this hearing is not about what Mr. Rogan may or may have not done wrong," said Standing.

"Mr. Standing, your function here is to represent the witness with regard to his constitutional rights. This is not a court of law, and we are not bound by any rules of evidence in our inquiry. Are you instructing your client not to answer the question?"

"No, Mr. Chairman, I am merely pointing out that the question is irrelevant."

"Your objection is noted, Mr. Standing. Now, Mr. Rogan, please answer the question."

"Sometimes rules have to be broken for the greater good. If Nazi generals had done that during World War II, perhaps millions of innocent people would not have been slaughtered like pigs," said Seth.

"Order!" said the Chairman. "Your answer is non-responsive."

"That's why I broke the rules, Senator, because Germinat, with the FDA's and EPA's help, intended to harm innocent citizens of this country with genetically engineered foods that they knew were unsafe. I exposed the reports to help my fellow Americans, not to betray them."

"Order!" barked the Chairman. "The Chair recognizes the distinguished Senator from Iowa."

"Mr. Rogan, I understand you are concerned with genetically engineered foods, but these hearings are about government corruption, not agriculture," said the distinguished Senator.

"Senator, without government corruption, none of these foods would have been approved," said Seth.

" What do you mean?"

"I think you know how it works, Senator. The big chemical companies fill the coffers of one of your colleagues who is a lawmaker from an agricultural state such as, well, let's take Iowa for example, and the lawmaker recommends the President install industry executives in high positions, such as the head of the FDA or the EPA. This way, the industry can approve its own products without safety testing."

"That is not responsive to my question," said the Senator.

"Order!" yelled the Chairman, pounding his gavel. "You are speaking out of turn."

"I haven't finished my answer yet, Mr. Chairman. These appointees are supposed to work for the people. Instead, they have held back facts and covered up deficiencies that they had a duty to disclose. When I tried to expose this corruption, they sent agents of the government after me to try to kill me. If that is not government corruption, then I don't know what is."

"Mr. Rogan, this technology has been known to be safe for many years," said the distinguished Senator from Iowa. "It's important to have this technology to save the world from starvation."

"Sir, if this technology is allowed to continue without proper testing, there will be no more world to feed. The doctors at the FDA and the EPA's own scientists have been telling the government and Germinat for years that the technology was not safe, and that further testing was warranted. The FDA, under the direction of Germinat employees, was urged to take the company's word for it instead of insisting on further testing. Then they tell the people that the government performs extensive safety testing on these food products. It is not true!"

"Order!" yelled the Chairman, pounding his gavel. "That will be enough, Mr. Rogan."

"Let him finish the answer," said Standing.

"My own tests conclude that the Bt toxin in GMO foods breach the digestive system and cause intestinal lesions and pre-cancerous cells. We already have an epidemic of diabetes and cancers of all kinds. There are studies linking GMO foods to obesity, cancer, diabetes, digestive problems, allergies, attention deficit disorder, and even gluten intolerance. Kids are even getting diabetes, which is unheard of in countries where there are no GMOs. There are GMOs in baby formulas, for God's sake. If you don't stop this now, you are going to have a generation of Americans with obesity, diabetes, colon cancer, babies with brain cancer, and that's not including all the cancers, birth defects, and sterilization from glyphosate poisoning from the non-Bt GMOs. This epidemic will make DDT and thalidomide look like Halloween candy compared to GMO foods."

"Well, sir, obviously we have two sides to the story; yours, the word of a person who stole top-secret government reports and went off to Russia, and scientific reports which say that these foods are just as safe as conventional ones."

"Those reports are not based on any human or even animal testing. They are made by the industry. Germinat is telling the government that its products are safe, and the government takes its word for it. We have to send a clear message to Congress that the people of the United States are not for sale."

"That will be all, Mr. Rogan," said the Chairman. "You are excused."

"How about doing the job we hired you gentlemen and ladies for? Start doing it by reading the legislation you pass. If you don't know what it says, don't vote for it."

"Mr. Rogan, if you don't stand down, you will be found in contempt," said the Chairman.

"Stop passing laws to benefit the chemical companies by sneaking them in on bills that nobody reads and pass some legislation that helps prevent corruption in powerful political appointments. If you want to stop corruption, pass laws limiting your terms in office and prohibiting you from taking jobs in the private sector for a reasonable time after you leave office."

"Mr. Rogan!" said the Chairman. "You are dangerously close to being held in contempt."

"The FDA and the EPA are supposed to be protecting us, not the people who make the poison."

The hearing went on for days, with Seth being ushered to and from the Capitol building by armed U.S. Marshals. Finally, his part was done, and he could resume his life in the place he had selected as his choice.

Blame always has to be assigned and punishment meted out. Watergate has taught people in power to allow others lower on the totem pole to suffer for the common good. Bill Penner was dismissed from his position at the FDA and indicted. The EPA's Richard Roberts suffered a similar fate, but the real culprit, Germinat, was spared and business continued as usual. This was far from a solution to the problem. You can't kill a snake unless you cut off the head.

CHAPTER 61

The waves lapped up against the sunny black sand beach as Seth kicked back in his chaise lounge on the balcony of his new house on the sunny Kona coast of Hawaii. While he relaxed, Natasha emerged from the beach house with two drinks.

"Care for an aperitif?" she asked, handing him a tequila sunrise.

"Yes, I would." She put her drink down on the table and sat in the lounge next to his to watch the spectacular sunset.

"Not a lot going on here," she said.

"It's the perfect place to hide."

"How do you figure that?"

"It's away from everything, everywhere. I have a new identity and a new job - nothing to take me back to that dangerous life."

"I'm not sure I want our kids to grow up here. It's so isolated."

"We can go wherever you want. As soon as my trail cools down, we'll travel the world until we find the right place."

Natasha smiled and said, "Scoot over," moving onto Seth's chaise. "I'm not so sure about that," she said, stroking his hair and cuddling next to him. "At least, not for now."

"What do you mean?"

"I heard that 90% of papayas are GMO, and they grow them right here. I also heard that the native Hawaiians have just burned several acres of papaya trees in protest."

"And?"

"They obviously need a voice."

"I'm not sure I like where you're going with this."

"Well, you stood up on the soapbox, not I. They're even asking for you by name."

Seth looked around at the naturally growing papaya trees and palm trees surrounding his house and thought, once again, about the ecosystem. Was he the only one in the world who cared?

Focusing on your own narrow needs creates apathy, which holds no benefits for anyone. The bait on a hook is always free, and sometimes, if you're lucky, you can take it without being caught, but you will always be a puppet on someone else's line if you don't care enough about the big picture to let your tiny voice be heard. When it is combined with the tiny voices of millions of others, that is the real power.

AFTERWORD

This is a work of fiction, but the threat is real. Genetically engineered foods are in almost all processed food products in the United States. A simple reading of the label will reveal one or more of the following ingredients in every one of them: corn or corn oil, cottonseed oil, canola oil (made from rapeseed oil, a GMO product), soy and/or soybean oil, and/or high fructose corn syrup.

Genetically engineered corn and soy are used for most of the animal feed in the United States, and GMO sweet corn is now appearing in stores. There are no current federal labeling laws for GMO products, and two labeling measures in California and Washington have been defeated in the wake of heavy spending of millions of dollars against the measures by Monsanto, Dow Chemical, Bayer, Coca Cola, Kellogg's, and many others whose names you will see on products on your breakfast, lunch or dinner table. A member of the board of directors of McDonald's and one from Sara Lee sit on the board of directors of Monsanto.

The classified report on biological warfare in the story is fictitious (at least none has been disclosed), but the government reports cited from scientists at the FDA, EPA and USDA reporting GMOs as unsafe and calling for toxicology reports and further testing are real, having been accessed through litigation using the Freedom of Information Act. You can read about them on the Internet. Arpad Pusztai is a real scientist who conducted the first experiments on lab rats and whose work was severely discredited until the UK government found out the real truth; that it had rushed into early approval of

GMO foods, and its ministers had hired Pusztai to do the study in two weeks after already having approved GMO foods for public consumption.

Since chemical companies invented genetically engineered seeds designed to withstand heavy sprayings of glyphosate, global use of Roundup and related weed killers has jumped to nearly 900 million pounds annually. That is due to the fact that, since the crops are engineered to be resistant to Roundup, it can be sprayed on the entire field, not just on the weeds, making it much easier for farmers to manage weed kills. Glyphosate is a systemic chemical meaning, once sprayed, it travels up inside the plants that people and animals eat, and they consume the glyphosate as well as the nutrients in the plants. As more farm fields have converted to GMO crops, federal regulators at the EPA (and former employees of Monsanto) have quietly allowed an increase in the levels of glyphosate allowed in our food, something from which we should see tragic, long-term consequences.

According to Stephanie Seneff, PhD, senior research scientist at Massachusetts Institute of Technology's Computer Science and Artificial Intelligence Laboratory, glyphosate acts as a potent bacteria killer in the gut, wiping out delicate beneficial microflora that helps protect us from disease. Harmful pathogens like Clostridium botulinum, Salmonella, and E. coli are able to survive glyphosate in the gut, but the "good bacteria" in your digestive tract, such as protective microorganisms, bacillus and lactobacillus, are killed off.

Even Monsanto knows about this. About 10 years ago, the company registered a patent for glyphosate's use as an antimicrobial agent. This damage to your digestive system can cause other problems, including "leaky gut," where the protective lining of the gut is compromised, allowing for toxins and bacteria to enter the bloodstream. This causes the body to send off an immune response to attack the wayward bacteria, potentially sparking autoimmune diseases.

Moreover, glyphosate interferes with tryptophan, the precursor of serotonin, an important neurotransmitter linked to happiness and well-being. Low serotonin levels have been linked to suicide, depression, obsessive-compulsive disorder, and other ailments. Not only does glyphosate hamper tryptophan production in your gut, it also lowers levels of it in plants, causing even more of a deficiency.

Virtually all of the genetically engineered (GMO) Bt corn grown in the U.S. is treated with neonicotinoid pesticides. A 2012 study found high levels of clothianidin in pneumatic planter exhaust. In the study, it was found that the insecticide was present in the soil of unplanted fields nearby those planted with Bt corn and also on dandelions (a favorite of bees) growing near those fields. Once in the soil, the pesticide remains for many years and is absorbed by any new plant life.

The Bt toxin, which was the subject of Seth's study in the story, essentially pokes "holes" in the cells of insects' stomachs, killing them and has been found to poke holes in human cells as well. In one study, it was found in the blood of 93% of pregnant women tested and in the blood of 80% of their unborn fetuses, which gets into the brains of the fetuses due to the fact that there is no blood-brain barrier at that stage of development.

Peer reviewed studies are rare in the case of GMOs because the only ones who have the desire or the budget to perform them are the same chemical companies that fund most of the scientific research. However, the few independent studies that have been done all point to the danger of GMOs.

Specificity of the association of GMO foods and specific disease processes is also supported. Multiple animal studies show significant immune dysregulation, including upregulation of cytokines associated with asthma, allergy, and inflammation. Animal studies also show altered structure and function of the liver, including altered lipid and carbohydrate metabolism, as well as cellular changes that could lead to accelerated aging. Changes in the kidney, pancreas, and spleen have also been documented.

A recent 2008 study links Bt corn with infertility, showing a significant decrease in offspring over time and significantly lower litter weight in mice fed Bt corn. American pig farmers have reported infertility and false pregnancies in their livestock after feeding them Bt corn. The study also found that over 400 genes were found to be expressed differently in mice fed Bt corn. These are genes known to control protein synthesis and modification, cell signaling, cholesterol synthesis, and insulin regulation. Studies also show intestinal damage in animals fed GMO foods, including proliferative cell growth and disruption of the intestinal immune system.

Because of this mounting data, it is biologically plausible for genetically modified foods to cause adverse health effects in humans. In spite of this risk, the biotech industry claims that GMO foods can feed the world through production of higher crop yields. However, a recent report by the Union of Concerned Scientists reviewed 12 academic studies and indicates otherwise: "The several thousand field trials over the last 20 years for genes aimed at increasing operational or intrinsic yield (of crops) indicate a significant undertaking. Yet none of these field trials have resulted in increased yield in commercialized major food/feed crops, with the exception of Bt corn." However, it was further stated that the increase in yields was largely due to traditional breeding improvements.

Therefore, because GMO foods pose a serious health risk in the areas of toxicology, allergy and immune function, reproductive health, and metabolic, physiologic and genetic health and are without any of their claimed benefits, the American Academy of Environmental Medicine (AAEM) believes that it is imperative to adopt the precautionary principle. It is one of the main regulatory tools of the European Union environmental and health policy and serves as a foundation for several international agreements. The most commonly used definition is from the 1992 Rio Declaration that states: "In order to protect the environment, the precautionary approach shall be widely applied by States according to their capabilities. Where there are threats of serious or irreversible damage, lack of full scientific certainty shall not be used as a reason for postponing cost-effective measures to prevent environmental degradation."

The FDA does not test the safety of GMO crops. Instead, all GMO foods are assumed to be safe unless there is already evidence to the contrary. The FDA relies on self-reported data from the companies that manufacture the crops as to their safety. Moreover, due to legal and copyright restrictions surrounding GMO patents, independent scientists must ask for the chemical companies' permission before publishing research on their products. As a result, almost all of the long-term animal feeding studies that have ever been conducted on GMO feed have been carried out by the biotech companies themselves, with their own rules and using their own standards of reporting. What few independent studies have been conducted have shown a range of adverse health effects from reduced fertility to immune system dysfunction, liver failure, obesity and cancer.

The revolving door between big agriculture, the FDA, the USDA and the EPA is also true. In a classic case of revolving door politics, the Obama administration's Deputy Commissioner of Foods, Michael Taylor, refuses to make FDA testing of GMO food safety mandatory. Taylor worked for the FDA from 1976 to 1981, when he went into private practice at a law firm that represented Monsanto, only to return through the revolving door to the FDA in 1991. In 1988, he published an article entitled "The De Minimis Interpretation of the Delany Clause: Legal and Policy Rationale" in the Journal of the American College of Toxicology (now called the International Journal of Toxicology). He had previously presented this article in December 1986 at a symposium on Topics in Risk Analysis sponsored by International Life Sciences Institute Risk Science Institute, Society for Risk Analysis, and Brookings Institution. The paper was delivered and published during the midst of a debate and litigation over federal agencies' interpretation of the Delaney clause, a part of federal law written in 1958 that on its face, literally prohibits any chemical from being added, in any amount, to food that is processed, if that agent is carcinogenic.

As analytical instrumentation increased in power, and more and more agents were found to be carcinogenic at very low levels, the agencies had developed a quantitative risk assessment approach to interpreting the Delaney Clause. It stated that, if a carcinogen were present at levels less than 1 in 1,000,000 parts, the risk of that carcinogen was "de minimis," and it could be allowed on the market. In the article, Taylor presented arguments in favor of this approach. Advocates in favor of organic food have criticized Taylor for taking this stance and have attributed the stance not to a good-faith effort to reasonably regulate but to an alleged desire to benefit Monsanto financially.

Between 1994 and 1996, Taylor went back through the revolving door to the USDA where he acted as Administrator of the Food Safety & Inspection Service. During that term, he implemented a science-based approach to raising safety standards for meat and poultry production over the protests from industry, which has been called by food safety advocates "a truly heroic accomplishment" (but that was the only one). Between 1996 and 2000, after briefly returning to King & Spalding, he then returned to Monsanto to become Vice President for Public Policy. In 2009, Taylor, once again, returned to government through the revolving door as Senior Advisor to the FDA Commissioner and was appointed by President Obama on January 13, 2010, to another newly created post at the FDA - this time as Deputy Commissioner for Foods.

Former EPA head William Ruckelshaus spent two years on Monsanto's board of directors. Linda J. Fisher spent a decade working as Assistant Administrator of the EPA's Office of Pollution Prevention before leaving to head up Monsanto's lobbying team. Margaret Miller spent her time at Monsanto working on Monsanto's GMO bovine growth hormone and wrote the report on it that was submitted to the FDA before taking a job as Deputy Director of the FDA, where she approved her own report.

In July 2013, the EPA, under the leadership of former Monsanto employees, increased the allowable levels of glyphosate in food up to 100 ppm in animal feed and 40 ppm in oilseed crops and from 0.2 ppm to 3 ppm for sweet potatoes and 5 ppm in carrots (15 and 20 times the prior allowed rates).

The first version of GMO corn was attacked because it was found to be deadly to Monarch butterflies. That corn has been banned in Poland where it has been found to be a threat to bees.

Beta carotene-producing rice is being pushed in the Philippines, where neighbors near a Bt cornfield have already reported allergy and respiration problems. It is expected to be pushed in India as well, and Indonesia is taking steps to approve GMO corn and soy.

Finally, the world is now suffering from what seven out of ten biologists believe is a sixth mass extinction. The last mass extinction was 65 million years ago when the dinosaurs disappeared from the earth. This mass extinction is being caused by man. The use of non-renewable energy, pollution, deforestation, and the overuse of water and pesticides in agriculture are the primary culprits of what will be man's demise from the destruction of his environment. We will kill off everything that lives on the earth now, but nature will come back - this time without us, and maybe that's a good thing for the planet.

One more thing...

I hope you have enjoyed this book and I am thankful that you have spent the time to get to this point, which means that you must have received something from reading it. I would be honored if you would post your thoughts, and also leave a review.

Best regards,
Kenneth Eade
info@kennetheade.com

CONTINUE THE ADVENTURES OF THE INVOL-
UNTARY SPY IN "TO RUSSIA FOR LOVE"

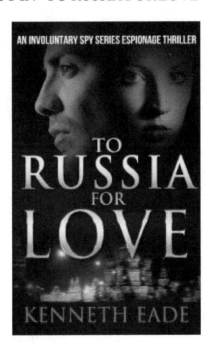

CHAPTER ONE

Seth Rogan woke up with a feeling that something was wrong this morning. In fact, he had woken up on the wrong side of the bed every morning for the past three weeks, since his girlfriend, Natalia Andropova (nicknamed Natasha) had not been in it. It had been very comfortable in this Hawaiian paradise as long as she had been here, but now she was gone and the room seemed empty – home was not home anymore.

Natasha's boss had called and had sent her on a special assignment. That boss was none other than Vladimir Putin, arguably the most, or second most, powerful man in the world. Natasha served as an undercover agent for the Russian Federal Security Service, the FSB – the successor to the old KGB.

Seth had woken up in a foul mood every day since she had left, and for the first time since he had settled in this island paradise, he was bored. It didn't make sense. Who could be bored with a beautiful house on the Kona Coast of the Big Island of Hawaii? He had his biological research to keep him busy, and he talked to her on the phone every day. Still it was not the same.

Since she had left, the first order of business was the telephone, something that Seth normally found to be a nuisance. Natasha was in Moscow presently, which was 14 hours ahead of Hawaii, so hers was the voice that Seth woke up to every morning and the one that put him to bed, but he had not heard from her in four days, and that made sleeping more of a chore than a necessity.

He had spent his waking hours, which were expanding due to his worries, calling her cell phone and leaving messages, texting an emailing, but Natasha had not responded. That was not like her, as she had been regularly checking in with him. Something was not right.

Seth looked at the clock. 9:30 already. *That's odd, by now she should have called.* Five minutes later, the phone rang. He rolled over and grabbed the phone.

"Hey baby."

"Seth, it's me – Abramov. The voice of Boris Abramov was a familiar one; one he knew from the days when he had lived undercover in Russia.

"Boris, I thought you were Natasha. I'm so glad you called."

"She's missing Seth."

"Missing?" Seth's heart surged as if it would jump out of his throat. "What are you talking about?"

"Someone has put out an anonymous missing persons report. We are looking for her."

Seth was in a panic. He could not think. He got up from his bed and paced the floor.

"But Natasha's supposed to be in Moscow."

"She arrived in Kiev two weeks ago. She was to attend agricultural conference."

"I know, I know, I was going to the same conference. But the conference was in Moscow. Why was she in Kiev?"

"They sent her there on assignment."

"What kind of assignment?"

"I can't talk about it over phone. Can you come to Kiev?"

"I'll be on the next plane. How do I reach you?"

"Not me. You will meet Victor Godinov, our man with Russian Embassy."

"What about the police? Are they working on it?"

"They say they are – Detective Ivan Petrenko is in charge of case. I'm not sure what help he may be, but I would like you to be on ground in Kiev in case we need you – in case Natasha needs you."

"Of course, I'm there."

Seth frantically wrote down the information, fired up his laptop, and booked a ticket to Kiev. It was over 21 hours of flying with layovers in San Francisco and Munich – 21 hours more that Natasha would be missing, and every second of that would count.

CHAPTER TWO

On the way to the airport, Seth's mind was racing. *Was she still alive?* The feeling of helplessness was paralyzing, but once he got on the ground in Kiev, hopefully that situation would change for the better. Seth looked at his cell phone. Suddenly, he received a cryptic text message from Natasha. *Now, at least something.* The message read: *I am the Captive Knight.*

What did it mean?

He tried calling back, but there was no answer. He texted. All the way to the airport, he frantically dialed her number, over and over again, to no avail.

Natasha had invited Seth to give a talk at an international agricultural conference on genetically engineered foods. Contrary to the United States, Russia had enacted legislation requiring GMO labeling and safety testing. There was a ban on the import of genetically engineered foods and they would not be introduced into the environment unless and until significant studies had been completed in the future.

Seth was called to the conference as an expert on GMOs. As a biologist who had worked for Germinat, the largest biotech company in the world, he had discovered a lot of information during his tenure at the company which had convinced him that the current technologies were not safe at all, and the absence of any safety testing by the FDA was undeniably negligent, in his opinion.

Ukraine had similar legislation but, even in the face of that, Germinat had established offices there, had invested $140 million in a non-GMO seed plant, and was in the midst of a "social development program" which offered rural Ukrainians up to

$25,000 in grants to provide educational opportunities, community empowerment and small business development. The company had also purchased large amounts of farm land in Ukraine, known for its rich soil and agricultural importance as Europe's "bread basket." Seth knew that his former employer had no interest in the social development of Ukraine or in producing non-GMO seeds. It was a chemical company, whose strategy in seed development was to develop seeds for crops that would resist its famous pesticide, *Cleanup,* or (as in the project Seth had worked on for the company) crops that generated their own pesticides.

Seth kept calling Natasha's number until the flight attendant told him to turn off his phone. After the plane took off, Seth fired up his laptop and studied the reports he had downloaded from the Internet. He picked at his meal while reading, then finally dozed off.

The waves lapped gently against the black sand beach as Seth watched Natasha emerge from the ocean, smiling. She ran up to him, dripping water onto his sun-soaked body. The drops were soothing, but not as cold as the intermittent rain showers that he had gotten so used to during their days on the Big Island. Seth tackled her onto the blanket.

"Careful! You'll break the shell!"

She produced from her hand a beautiful pink conch shell.

"I just found it. Isn't it beautiful?"

Seth looked at the shell, then Natasha's innocent looking, young face. She had been through more than anyone should have this past year and a half. Originally introduced to him as a 20-something English teacher right out of the university, she had an air of maturity about her that made her wiser than her years.

Perhaps that was why they had enlisted her in the Federal Security Service. Nobody would suspect this innocent looking, exquisite creature was really an undercover agent.

Seth woke up with a warm feeling, only to realize that it had only been a dream. He reached into his pocket and pulled out the conch shell and felt its smooth surface against his fingers. For the past six months they had spent their days in the endless summer of the islands of Hawaii, exploring each hidden waterfall and deserted beach. During that time, their budding romance (which had started when they had met in Russia) had bloomed into a full blown relationship, and Seth's single days no longer had a place in his memory. It was as if he was another person then, and as though Natasha had always been in his life.

The reports Seth reviewed indicated that Ukraine had entered into an agreement with the European Union, which paved the way for $17 billion in aid from the International Monetary Fund. This agreement contained a little-known clause about the development of biotechnology which committed Ukraine to cooperate to "extend the use of biotechnologies." It may as well have said that Ukraine would agree to allow the production of genetically engineered foods.

Seth was not an investigator, but had (more or less) been forced into that role when he had worked for Germinat. During that experience, he had developed a full blown "secret agent" toolset, not out of desire as much as out of necessity. Those skills helped him, at first, to steal crucial records from his employer which exposed the dangers of their genetically engineered foods, and later those same skills saved his life.

The United States had put $5 billion into the opposition that ousted President Yanukovych from office and forced him to flee to Russia, and had planted their own operatives into key business and government positions in Ukraine after the election of the new president, Petro Poreshenko, who, Seth learned, had been an informant for the United States since 2006. In April 2014, Vice President Joe Biden's son, Hunter Biden, and Devon Archer, a close friend of Secretary of State John Kerry, had been appointed to the board of directors of Ukraine's largest natural gas producer. The U.S. State Department's Natalie Jaresko had also been transplanted into the Ukrainian government as their Finance Minister, and was granted Ukrainian citizenship on the day of her appointment.

As Seth looked at all the pieces, Natasha's disappearance began to make sense. He didn't know what her undercover assignment had been, but if it was in Ukraine, it had to have something to do with the current unrest going on there. And she wasn't just missing-she was in real danger.

CHAPTER THREE

After passing through customs and border control, Seth saw, on his right, a man holding a sign with the name "Rogan." He was about 28, nicely dressed in a conservative suit, and appeared to be Russian. To his left, two American-looking businessmen, conservatively dressed in suits in different shades of grey, stood with another man who appeared to be their driver. They made eye contact with him, and he understood that they were also waiting for him. A tinge of panic tingled his cerebral cortex as he recalled the last greeting he had had in this country, which was not so welcoming. Hopefully this one would be less dramatic. One of the men in the suits approached him.

"Mr. Rogan?" he asked, in a perfect American accent.

Seth ignored him and approached the driver holding the sign.

"Hello, Mr. Rogan," said the driver, in a strong Russian accent. "I am Victor Godinov from Russian Embassy. I have instructions from Ambassador to bring you safely to embassy."

Seth looked over his shoulder. The two suits were watching them. He shook Godinov's hand, and Godinov took his small carry-on suitcase.

"Nice to meet you, Godinov."

"For me too, sir. We should probably hurry."

Seth matched Godinov's quick pace as they exited the arrivals area with the two suits and their driver not far behind.

At curbside, a black Mercedes 600 pulled up.

"This is our car, sir, please..."

Seth got in, and looked behind him to see the two suits also getting into a black Mercedes land cruiser. As the 600 pulled out and accelerated, the land cruiser followed. But, just after the 600 took off, an old blue Volga pulled out into the lane, blocking the land cruiser's pursuit. The Volga puffed out a large plume of black smoke as it stalled in the middle of the lane. Seth could hear the horn of the land cruiser blazing as he looked through the rear window.

"We made sure this time your airport transfer would be more comfortable," said Victor. Seth could see by now that Victor was obviously an FSB agent. It wasn't long before the black Mercedes was securely behind the gates of the Russian Embassy.

***

Seth sat in the familiar waiting room where he had began his first excursion into espionage long ago. It looked like a museum, with its classic oil paintings, richly wallpapered walls and antique French furniture. He looked at his cell phone to see if there were any emails from Natasha or the police, but there was no signal.

"It won't work here," said Victor as he entered the waiting room. "Secure area. We will give you Wi-Fi code to use."

"Thank you."

The door to the Ambassador's office opened and they were beckoned in by a beautiful blonde girl. The Ambassador rose to greet them, extending his hand, which Seth took in his.

"Ambassador Petrov, it's good to see again you, sir."

"Likewise, Mr. Rogan, but I'm afraid that this time is a little more dangerous than the last."

"Hard to imagine that, sir," said Seth, as he and Victor sat down in front of the Ambassador's desk.

"Mr. Rogan, Victor here is one of our best men. He is in charge of the investigation for Miss Andropova, and he will give you a full briefing on what we know and what we don't know."

"Thank you both," said Seth.

"But you must let us handle this," said the Ambassador. "You don't know this country and, as you probably have realized by now, the CIA already knows you are here. It is not safe for you."

"With all due respect, sir, I have been in these situations before, and..."

"You are in over head here," interrupted Godinov.

"Victor, please," said the Ambassador. "Let me explain. Since the coup that ousted President Yanukovych, things have been on a heightened alert here and in Russia. There is an escalating civil war that the current government of the United States wants nothing more than to blame on Russia to advance the business interests of their own oligarchy."

"Yes, I've been reading about this."

"The oligarchy in control of Ukraine has many American business partners. The Minister of Finance is from the U.S. State Department. The last time you were here, there was less of a CIA presence. Now, they are everywhere."

"You can't trust police, or anybody, right now," said Victor. "Please, let us handle situation."

"Victor, you're talking about my girl. She's not a situation. How did she get involved in the first place? She was working on agriculture."

"We cannot discuss her assignment," said Victor.

"American agriculture has a big stake here," said the Ambassador. "John Deere, and your company, Germinat – they have a lot to gain here, especially with a government that will do whatever they want."

"My ex-company," Seth interjected.

"We think Miss Andropova got too close. Hopefully, she is just too far undercover to communicate and they have not exposed her as FSB agent," said Victor.

"But what does her message mean?" asked Seth.

"It's a poem by Lermontov," said Victor. "Called *Captive Knight*. In it, the knight describes his prison. We think she was trying to indicate to you that she had been taken captive."

"But why use a poem; why not just say it?"

"Maybe to disguise message. Maybe because she didn't have time to leave proper message. They were most likely monitoring her communications," said Victor. "She must have sent message on her phone before they took it."

"Mr. Rogan, you are free to do as you choose," said the Ambassador. "But both your safety and that of Miss Andropova depends on you letting us take the lead on this."

"If you can't even discuss her assignment with me, how can I trust you? She may be your agent, but she's my *life*."

"We understand," said the Ambassador. "You have to trust that we are doing everything in our power to locate Miss Andropova."

"But what if that's not enough?"

"We are dealing with very bad people," said Victor. "Same ones who glorify role of Nazi partisans in World War II and call them "freedom fighters." The fascist parties of Ukraine have gained lot of power recently, and they have their own members already in government. You have to let us do our job and stay out of way."

"I can handle myself."

"They know you are here. You stick out like big thumb," said Victor.

"Sore thumb."

"Yes, sore thumb. By spying around, you will only bring danger to Natalia."

"Look, I will lay low for now. But, let me ask you something, Mr. Ambassador. If it was your wife who was missing, would you just sit by idly and do nothing?"

Petrov looked at Seth and frowned. "I see your point, Mr. Rogan. But I am afraid that national security must take a front seat to your personal interests. I am sorry. Victor will give you as much information as he can on the case. Then, you will be on your own. "

Petrov rose and extended his hand, which Seth took in his. "Please stay in close communication with us. We may need you."

OTHER BOOKS BY KENNETH EADE
Brent Marks Legal Thriller Series
A Patriot's Act
Predatory Kill
HOA Wire
Unreasonable Force
Killer.com
Absolute Intolerance
The Spy Files
Decree of Finality
Beyond All Recognition
The Big Spill
And Justice?
Involuntary Spy Espionage Series
An Involuntary Spy
To Russia for Love
Stand Alone
Terror on Wall Street
Paladine Political Thriller Series
Paladine
Russian Holiday
Traffick Stop
Unwanted

ABOUT THE AUTHOR

Described by critics as "one of our strongest thriller writers on the scene," author Kenneth Eade, best known for his legal and political thrillers, practiced International law, Intellectual Property law and E-Commerce law for 30 years before publishing his first novel, "An Involuntary Spy." Eade, an award-winning, best-selling Top 100 thriller author, has been described by his peers as "one of the up-and-coming legal thriller writers of this generation." He is the 2015 winner of Best Legal Thriller from Beverly Hills Book Awards and the 2016 winner of a bronze medal in the category of Fiction, Mystery and Murder from the Reader's Favorite International Book Awards. His latest novel, "Paladine," a quarter-finalist in Publisher's Weekly's 2016 BookLife Prize for Fiction and finalist in the 2017 RONE Awards. Eade has authored three fiction series: The

"Brent Marks Legal Thriller Series", the "Involuntary Spy Espionage Series" and the "Paladine Anti-Terrorism Series." He has written eighteen novels which have been translated into French, Spanish, Italian and Portuguese.